W9-DEE-345

JUST LIKE EVERYBODY ELSE

JUST LIKE EVERYBODY ELSE

LILLIAN ROSEN

Harcourt Brace Jovanovich, Publishers
San Diego   New York   London

Copyright © 1981 by Lillian D. Rosen

Requests for permission to make copies of any part of the work should be mailed to: Permissions, Harcourt Brace Jovanovich, Inc., 757 Third Avenue, New York, New York 10017.

Printed in the United States of America

LIBRARY OF CONGRESS CATALOGING IN PUBLICATION DATA
Rosen, Lillian.
Just like everybody else.
SUMMARY: Fifteen-year-old Jenny struggles to resume a normal life following an accident that leaves her deaf.
    [1. Deaf—Fiction. 2. Physically handicapped—Fiction] I. Title.
PZ7.R71866Ju   [Fic]   81–47534
ISBN 0–15–241652–8   AACR2

C D E

To my son, Eric,
and
to "different" youngsters everywhere

JUST LIKE EVERYBODY ELSE

1

■ Until that cruel winter day I figured I was one of the lucky ones. At almost sixteen, I'd known mostly good things.

I lived in Millport, a small, pretty city in Connecticut. I had two special friends and reasonably decent parents. True, they were impossible sometimes, but I knew they loved me even if we did have trouble communicating now and then. I'd often wished I had a brother or sister. I did have a beautiful blue-gray cat called Smokey.

School was bearable that year. If I wasn't exactly a social butterfly, at least I had hopes. Some of the guys had gotten friendlier recently, as if they had finally discovered that girls are people, too. At lunch that day Dan Martino had finally asked me to the end-of-the-term dance. He sure took his time! I'd almost given up hoping one of the guys would ask me. Last year nobody did.

The last thing I remembered before the whole world and everyone in it disappeared was getting on the bus and trying to find Donna and Nancy to tell them about Dan. Then someone screamed, and I blacked out.

When I opened my eyes, everything around me was white and shiny plastic and glass. The bed I was lying on was stiff and hard. I turned my head gingerly. A tall pole with an inverted plastic bottle hanging from its top stood to the left of my bed. Extending from the bottle was a long, slender tube. The end of it was attached to my left arm under a wide rubber cuff.

That had to be an IV setup. The fluid in the tube must be going into my veins. I was obviously in a hospital. Why? Nothing hurt anywhere. Slowly I lifted my head, slid my right arm and hand down along my body, and wiggled my toes. Then I gently lifted first one leg, then the other. All there, and everything worked. Good! I put my hand to my face and then touched my head. I checked my nose, face, mouth, eyes—all there, no bandages. I felt awfully groggy, and there were strange noises inside my head. My fingers found a stiff bandage on my hair on the right side. My palm covered it.

Ugh! I must have hit my head! But I didn't feel any pain even there. Had they given me drugs? Was that why there was no pain?

A hand suddenly touched mine very gently. I looked up at a blond woman in white uniform and cap. She smiled at me and mumbled something I couldn't quite catch.

"Hey! Nothing hurts. What am I doing here? What's happened? Where's my mother? Why am I in a hospital? What's wrong with me?"

She patted my hand again, mumbled something else, then pressed a button and spoke into a machine. She spoke—I could see her lips move—but I couldn't hear what she said!

"Hey! Could you talk louder, please?" I asked, frowning. My voice wasn't coming out right either. It felt strange. I couldn't hear what *I* was saying. Suddenly Mom and Dad appeared. Mom reached out and hugged me close while Dad grabbed my hand. At their side stood a slim man in white. He took my other hand gently. I saw the question on his face—he had to be asking how I felt, but . . .

"I feel okay, I guess, except my head feels awfully funny. And . . . I can't hear you! I can't hear any of you! What's wrong, why can't I *hear* you?"

Eyebrows rose; lips moved quickly and inaudibly. Suddenly a small pad appeared in the doctor's hands, and he scribbled furiously. When he finished, he showed me the pad.

"You've been in an accident, Jenny. You hit the right side of your head very hard. You've fractured your skull."

"What accident?" I asked.

"The school bus skidded on an icy patch of road," he wrote. "It hit the side of a tree, and you banged your head against a metal pole. It knocked you out."

"For how long?"

"You've been unconscious for over forty-eight hours."

"Oh! Are the others kids okay, Mom?"

"They're fine, love," she assured me.

The doctor took the pad from her and wrote quickly again. "The right side of your skull took the full impact. How do you feel? Does your head hurt?"

"It doesn't hurt exactly. It's just that there are noises inside my head—ringing, ticking, and bells, even a cymbal clangs every so often. It's weird and hard to describe!"

"You're doing it very well!" he scribbled on the pad. "What else?"

"Well . . . wait a minute. What's your name? Who are you?"

"I'm sorry, Jenny, I forgot my manners. I'm Dr. Corwin. I'm an otologist. That's just a fancy name for a specialist in ear, nose, and throat problems. I'm also a surgeon. Your family doctor, Dr. Golden, called me as soon as he had examined you."

"Oh, that's good, I guess. When will I be able to hear again? Are you going to operate?"

I looked at him more closely as he scribbled. Gee, he was good-looking! Sandy hair, blue eyes, and a warm smile. He looked awfully young to be a surgeon! I suddenly wished I were ten years older and not so skinny.

"We're not sure, Jenny. We have to take more tests, X-rays of your brain and the bones inside your skull. Some are pretty complicated. We have to know more before we decide what to do, okay?"

"Sure. How long do I have to have this thing in my arm? And I'm hungry!"

He smiled broadly. "That's great!" he scribbled. "We'll put you back on regular food starting tomorrow morning. Meanwhile, you need lots of rest. Is there anything else you want?"

"Yes, please. May I see my friends? And could I have some books and magazines and a lipstick, please? Do I have to wear this awful hospital gown? Can I wear my own pajamas, please?"

The pen flew in response. "Yes, yes, of course, Jenny. Your mother can bring your own things in, and tomorrow you can have visitors. Now it's time to rest."

He patted my hand and grinned down at me. Mom leaned over and kissed me and squeezed my hand. They all left. The nurse smiled at me, too. I closed my eyes for a minute, and suddenly I felt very, very tired. The weird noises bothered me, but nothing really hurt.

I'll be okay, I guess, I told myself. And then I fell asleep.

2

■ The morning was bright and sunny. Anne, a chubby black nurse, who had the early shift, introduced herself, then dumped a dozen cards in my lap, from Donna and Nancy, from some of the kids at school, even from a couple of teachers. She showed me plants my aunt Betsy and uncle Harry and Donna's folks had sent. Then, at ten o'clock, an aide brought in a dozen red roses. The card read simply: "We love you so very much, Jenny! Mom and Dad." I buried my nose, my whole face in them, almost choking on the lump in my throat. Nobody had ever given me roses before.

Anne held out more cards: funny ones, sentimental ones—all bright and colorful, all telling me to hurry up and get well. There was one from Mr. Stein, my English teacher, even one from Old Eagle-Eye Crowley!

"Want to save them Jenny?" Anne wrote on the pad.

"Of course." My voice still didn't feel right. As I talked, it felt as if I was speaking from a very deep cavern far away. But people responded when I spoke, so I figured it must be coming out right to them.

Anne took a roll of tape and a stack of cards and marched over to the wall opposite my bed. Quickly, deftly, she taped up each card, spacing them carefully. When she finished, there was a parade of gay, colorful pictures marching across the white wall.

I felt like a fraud! I still wasn't hurting anywhere.

True, when I got up to go to wash or bathe, my legs would slide out from under me if Anne weren't there to hold me and walk with me. I was as wobbly as a baby just learning to walk! I wondered why. Both Dr. Corwin and Dr. Golden had been in to see me early in the morning. But I hadn't found out anything new from them.

Later Anne plopped me into a wheelchair and took me down to the lab, where a technician smiled, patted my head, and proceeded to smear my forehead with some kind of sticky cream. When it was just the way she wanted it, she attached a clamp with long wires fastened to it to the spots that were creamed. I felt weird with all those wires attached to my head! They led to a large metal box—that was all I could see. I would really have been scared except that Dr. Corwin had told me in the morning that I was scheduled for an EEG. They'd X-ray my brain, and it wouldn't hurt, he promised.

It didn't, but why did they have to do it? I wondered. Did they suspect brain damage? They must. They were nuts! My brain was okay, I was sure of that.

That afternoon, as soon as I knew school was out, I kept looking at my watch. Mom had brought me my prettiest pajamas, lipsticks, and my comb and brush. I had awakened from my after-lunch nap half an hour before and combed and brushed my hair (it was long, thank goodness, and covered my bandage). I looked reasonably decent, I thought, not very sick at all.

At a quarter to three Donna came bursting into the room. In one hand she held a bunch of mums, which she thrust into Anne's hands; in the other, a brown paper bag.

"Oh, Jenny, Jenny!" She leaned over and kissed and

hugged me, and we clung together for a minute. She pointed to the paper bag, and as I lifted out the contents, I grinned up at her, reached over, and gave her a hug.

The bag contained three of those little kids' magic pads—the ones you write on with a stick, then lift off the top plastic sheet and the writing disappears so you can write something else.

"Donna, they're perfect! You're a genius!" I exclaimed.

"They'll wear out, but I'll get you more when you need them," she wrote.

"Tell me what's happening, Donna, please. Tell me all the news. Did you go the dance? Who did Dan take? I've missed the final exams. Were they tough? Is Nancy coming, do you know? When?" I fired question after question at her, impatient even though she wrote quickly. She told me that she hadn't gone to the dance, that Nancy would visit; so would some of the other kids. We talked and talked, or rather I talked and she wrote. It felt so good to be with her again. The noises in my head didn't bother me now. I was hardly aware of them while she was with me.

Too soon Anne spoke to Donna, and she rose and kissed me quickly, then scribbled a last message on the magic pad: "Have to go, Jen. Mustn't get you too tired out. Be back soon. Love ya!"

After a last hug I watched her go. Then I leaned back, suddenly tired. Sweet, thoughtful, chubby Donna —constantly and sadly turning down the cakes and ice cream she loved (she said just looking at them added pounds). Strong, capable, and warm, with a smile that made everyone feel good. Always the first to defend the oddballs, fierce fighter against whatever she felt was unfair. Loving, loyal, always-there Donna. Thank God for Donna!

I closed my eyes just for a little while . . . When I opened them, Dottie, who took over the second shift at 4:00 P.M. was just coming in with the dinner tray. She cranked up the bed, plumped one pillow behind me, and tucked another under my knees. Everything smelled good, and I ate with my usual appetite. The thick soup, chicken, mashed potatoes, and squash disappeared quickly. The chocolate pudding I lingered over. Dottie grinned and shook her head. I knew what she was thinking. People always wondered how I could eat so much and never put on a pound.

Later Mom and Dad were suddenly there—everybody was always *suddenly* there now. I'd look up, feeling a touch on the hand or shoulder, startled for a minute. There had been no door opening or footsteps, no voice calling out, no way of knowing that certain things were happening. I was aware only of what I could see or touch or smell. When I spoke, I knew I was talking, but it still felt strange.

Mom and Dad and I talked, using the pad. They wrote cheering words, but I could see something else in their faces. They tried not to let it show, but they were worried, scared, too. I could tell. I didn't let myself think about it, though. I told myself parents were bound to be like that, worrying about even little things that happened to you. It figured that they'd be really upset at a time like this. Since they were determined to hide it, I decided to go along and play the game, too, for the time being anyway.

I told them about Donna's visit and all the cards people had sent. It was so good just to have them there and to know that one or both of them would be there every day. Being fussed over was super. I decided being "sick" had its advantages.

The next day, as soon as school was out, Nancy came, apologizing for not having come sooner. She dumped a large sketch pad and a dozen colored pencils into my lap. "For when you get tired of reading and talking," she scribbled on my pad.

I laughed. "Me? Get tired of talking? I was almost kicked out of kindergarten for talking so much."

Nancy giggled, and when Nancy giggled, you couldn't help laughing too. She always found the funny side of everything. It was she who decided Miss Crowley looked like an eagle searching for prey as she stalked through the classroom. That led to the nickname of Old Eagle-Eye. By the time Nancy left I felt a lot better.

After school on most days one or more of the kids from school stopped by. Dan Martino came once, too. One afternoon five kids came at the same time and started chattering away, mouths moving a mile a minute.

"Hey!" I yelled. "Hold it! I can't hear you, remember? Look, you decide which one of you is going to speak for all of you!" I handed over my pad and pencil. There was a brief conference. Then Tom, the editor of our school magazine, reached for the pad and scribbled: "Sorry, Jen! When are they going to fix your ear up?

How long before you can come back to school? We need you!"

When I read that, I almost cried. Instead, I took a deep breath and forced the words out. "I . . . I don't know, Tom. I feel stronger every day, and they keep checking me out, taking blood pressure and temps and tests of all kinds, but they keep stalling . . . I just don't know. . . ."

Now I felt scared, really scared. The five faces had stopped smiling at me. Tom drew his eyebrows together and scowled for a minute. Then he grabbed the pad and wrote quickly: "Okay. Take it easy, Jenny. These people know what they're doing. Takes time, I guess. You just hang in there, stay cool, and try not to worry. We'll manage. You're really doing fine; all the nurses say so. Look, how about if we run that poem of yours instead, since your story isn't finished. Unless you'd like to try to finish it up while you're here?"

"I'm not sure I can, Tom. Use the poem if you think it's good enough. The story may just have to wait . . ."

More scribbling. "Don't worry. We're all rooting for you! Even if they can't bring all your hearing back, you can always use a hearing aid. These new ones are very powerful. My uncle Bert wears one all the time. You can hardly see it!"

"I'm afraid no aid can help my left ear, Tom. I haven't heard a thing in that ear since I had a nasty ear infection when I was a kid."

The pad dropped from his fingers. His face was drawn with real concern as he spoke very, very slowly. "Jen . . . I, I never knew. . . ."

My eyes were glued to his face, to his slowly moving lips. I felt his shock. Then my whole body trembled as I yelled, "Tom, Tom, I understood you! You said you never knew, didn't you?"

"Jenny, you *heard* me!" he said, smiling and slowly pointing right at me, then to himself.

"No, no! I didn't *hear* you. I looked at your face and mouth and understood somehow. . . ."

His mouth moved quickly. This time I understood nothing. I saw Dottie's frowning face and moving lips, and suddenly it seemed as though everyone were talking at once. I couldn't understand a word. The whole scene reminded me of an old silent movie or a TV play when the audio is lost. I turned my head away and closed my eyes. It hurt so not to know what anyone was saying!

Tom took up the pad again. "Jen, your nurse thinks we'd better go now. I'll be back soon. We'll all come again if you want us to."

"If I *want* you to! Of course, I want you to. Please come again!" One of the girls, Ellen, leaned over and kissed me. Tom squeezed my hand and winked.

Dottie shooed them all out and wrote quickly: "Jen, are you all right?"

"Of course, I'm all right! I'm just a little shaky, that's all. Nothing like that has ever happened to me before. Dottie, I *understood* him! Just a few words, but I understood. I *did!*"

3

■ For the first time in weeks I started to think, really to think. I was feeling confused, excited, and frightened, all at the same time. There hadn't been time to think before, only time to react instinctively to situations and people—to eat and sleep and bathe and do what I was told to do unquestioningly. Now I decided it was time I faced the unasked questions. Why couldn't I hear? Could they restore my hearing? They had to! What were they doing anyway? I needed some answers. *Tonight,* I thought, *when Dr. Corwin comes to see me, I'll ask. I'll make him tell me the truth.* I had to. The tired feeling crept over me then, and I barely managed to get supper down before I fell asleep. When I opened my eyes, it was dark outside. The city looked pretty—all interwoven pinpoints of light against the darkening sky. Dottie was reading in the chair beside my bed.

"Hey, Dottie! Dr. Corwin hasn't come yet, has he?"

She shook her head. "No, but he'll be here. Soon," she wrote on my pad. "How do you feel? Want to sit up?"

"Yes, please. I'm okay, I guess. Could I have my comb and brush and a sip of juice, please, Dottie?"

Dottie cranked up the bed, plumped another fat pillow behind my back, and poured some juice for me. She smiled. The smile changed to a frown as she took the pad and scribbled. "What's the matter, puss? Head bothering you? You're awfully quiet. Not like you at all!" Then she added, "Scared, Jenny?"

"Oh, Dottie!" Not answering, I looked into her concerned face as she warmly placed her hand on mine. Beneath the crisp cap and uniform and the brisk, proper, no-nonsense approach there was always a special tenderness and awareness.

All the people coming day after day, all the flowers, the cards, even some letters (a beautiful one from Mr. Stein) touched me so. Everyone had been so kind I hadn't had time to be scared. They had kept me too busy!

Yet tonight I felt uneasy, apprehensive. It wasn't cold in the room, but I felt cold. I always enjoyed Dr. Corwin's visits, but tonight I could hardly wait for him to come. When would he come? He was late. Why *tonight?* My head was pounding. The drums were rumbling away, the swishing cymbals working overtime, the bells clanging . . .

I kept looking at the door, and finally, it was pushed open as my mother and father rushed in. They kissed me, flung off their coats, and apologized for being late. Why was it so important to be here at a certain time tonight? They came every night. The exact time varied. I always knew they would come; they knew that.

Before I could ask anything, they moved to sit close beside me, and then Dr. Corwin arrived and stood before me, the usual question on his lips. He looked tired but smiled gently his eyes searching my face.

"How's my girl feeling tonight?"

I took a deep breath. "Okay, same as usual. Look, this has been going on for weeks and weeks—testing, the examinations, the scribbling. When are you going to fix up my ear? When will I *hear* again?"

This time *he* took a deep breath, paused, and, as Dottie reached over and took my hands, wrote: "Jenny, your auditory nerve was destroyed when you hit your head. There is nothing we can do to bring back your hearing. I'm so sorry—" The pen almost fell from his hands.

I stared at the words on the pad for a few seconds. Then I flung it away and screamed, "No! Oh, God, *no! no!* No! No! No! It's not true! It can't be! You're crazy! It's a mistake!"

I stared at him. "You're saying I'm *deaf!* That I'll never hear anything or anybody *ever* again? There's no chance at *all?* Nothing you can do? *Nothing?*"

He nodded, his eyes bright with the tears he held back, but I couldn't hold back any longer.

Mom pulled me to her. I threw my arms around her and wept uncontrollably. My body shook. The tears streamed, the sobs almost choking me as we clung together, her face as wet as mine. That was all any of us could do then—cry. Just cry.

4

■ Deaf? Totally deaf? It just couldn't be. It didn't make any sense. Screwy things like this happened only to other people or maybe in stories or on TV or in nightmares. They didn't happen to *real* people like me. I wasn't even sixteen years old. Life, real life, was just beginning for me. I hadn't had a chance to live yet. If Dr. Corwin couldn't do anything, then maybe someone else could. He wasn't the only ear doctor in the world. He was wrong; he had to be wrong. This couldn't be happening to me. All I did was hit my head; I never hit my ear at all; there wasn't even a scratch on it!

I had cried, but I didn't believe what they said. If I didn't believe it, then it just wasn't so. Everything looked just the way it always had. People and places and things, I mean. They were all there, the same size and color and shape as they always had been.

I began to look more closely at people's faces, especially their mouths. I'd never really noticed how many differently shaped lips there were in the world. Now I noticed. I went through all the motions as they took still more tests. It was stupid, I thought, all this checking and rechecking, for brain damage, they said. There was absolutely nothing wrong with my brain; couldn't they see that at least? I knew who I was, where I was, who people were; I could read and talk and answer questions and ask them. What made them think there was any brain damage? And if they were wrong about that, if they couldn't be sure, how could they be sure there was nothing they could do to fix my ear? Doctors didn't know everything. They weren't gods. They were human beings, and human beings make mistakes. It wasn't hard to convince myself they had made a mistake. I just couldn't be deaf! Not for always.

One afternoon Dottie came in with a funny-looking thing made of curved metal tubes. Eyebrows lifted, I asked her what it was.

"It's a walker, Jenny," she scribbled. "You're getting to be a real lazy character, just sitting and sleeping all the time! Today we're going to take a walk down the hall. You need to exercise, pussycat. You want to walk again, don't you?"

"Sure, but I can walk. What do I need that thing for?"

"Ok, walk." Dottie gestured. "Come on." I swung my legs over the side of the bed and touched my feet to the floor. I felt awfully wobbly as usual, but I was determined to show her I didn't need her or the walker. I put my left foot out, took one step, and felt my knees start to buckle. If Dottie hadn't caught me, I would have collapsed completely. She slipped me back onto the edge of the bed and just looked at me. She placed the walker a foot from the bed. She didn't have to say anything; the words were written clearly on her face: "Okay, wise guy, now let's do it my way!"

"Okay, you win," I said.

She placed my hands on the bars and gestured "Up!" With the walker taking the weight of the upper part of my body, I tried again. First one step, then another, then lift the walker and repeat. Again and again and again. Slowly we moved out of the room and down the hall. At the end of the corridor we turned and walked back, then entered my room. Three steps from the bed, Dottie touched my arm; then, lifting my hands off the walker, she looked at me questioningly. I caught on and nodded my head. I'd take those last steps alone, without the walker. *Go, girl, go!* I told myself, and lunged forward. I made it. Gratefully I sank down on my beautiful, beautiful bed.

Dottie grinned. I knew she was pleased with me even before she scribbled on my pad. "You did very well, Jen. First time up is the hardest. It'll get easier. Soon you won't need the walker at all. Tomorrow we'll begin taking three walks a day!"

How could it be so hard to walk by myself? I thought. My legs knew what to do, and my mind sent out the right signals to my muscles; but they didn't respond very well. Was it all the weeks in bed? Probably. Still, I was puzzled.

I complained to Dr. Corwin that evening about feeling as if I were on a tightrope when I didn't use the walker. He explained that a severe hearing loss caused a loss of balance as well, since the inner ear controls balance. He assured me that once I was used to walking again, no one would ever notice.

"Dottie, what time is it?" I asked when Dr. Corwin left.

Instead of reaching for the pad and pen, she pulled a chair over to my bed, looked at me hard, then pointed to her lips, which moved slowly. I looked at her, puzzled.

"Oh, come on, Dottie," I complained, "you know I can't hear you."

Dottie gently put one hand on either side of my face and turned my head so that I was forced to look at her face. Her mouth moved again, and she held up two fingers, stopped, then moved once more a little bit faster, and she pointed to her wristwatch.

Oh, damn, what was she saying? What was she trying to do? Her lips moved again.

"Watch . . . lips . . . nine . . ." Suddenly I could understand.

"Watch my lips! It's nine o'clock!" I yelled, repeating what I saw her say and gesture. I could actually understand! "Dottie, oh, Dottie . . ." We were both grinning like idiots, and when Dottie grinned, the whole world lit up.

She grabbed the pad and wrote: "See? See? You can do it if you try hard enough!"

"But, Dottie, I don't really know how . . ." My voice faltered. It's hard to claim you don't know how to do something right after you've just done it.

We sat and looked at each other. By this time we knew each other pretty well. Dottie had scored again, I thought. I reached out for her hand, whispering gratefully, "Thanks, Dottie."

"Big deal! We've only made a beginning," she wrote, "but we'll keep at it. You caught on quickly."

From then on, every day that last week in the hospital, Dottie tried to talk to me a few times during her shift. Sometimes I could catch a word, a phrase, or a short sentence. Sometimes I couldn't. Mom and Dad tried it with me, too, when they came, but I rarely caught what they said. It upset them when I didn't, and me, too.

Dad promised me we would drive into New York in a few weeks to see another doctor, a man who'd invented an operation to cure one kind of deafness and had worked with hearing problems for ages. It had all been arranged. We had nothing to lose by getting another opinion.

I was glad when the day finally came to leave. It was hard to say good-bye to everyone, but I wanted badly to go home.

Dr. Corwin laid down a few last rules. He insisted that I shouldn't be left alone for the first months (we couldn't chance my falling and hitting my head) and that I should do as many things for myself as I could.

And so I left the comforting world of a regular routine, the cards and flowers, the constant attention and concern, the tender loving care of once total strangers. The drive home went quickly. Before I knew it, Mom was helping me out of the car, Dad unloading suitcases. After opening the door, Mom turned to bring in one of my plants.

After the first uneasy steps I wasn't frightened anymore and darted into the house. Where was Smokey? I called her, but she didn't come. I couldn't see her anywhere. Could she be sleeping out in the backyard? I moved quickly through the kitchen and opened the back door, stepped outside, and caught my breath, unbelieving, overwhelmed.

There had still been a few traces of snow on the ground weeks ago on the day I woke up in the hospital.

Now everything was a lush green, and before my eyes was a rich golden blaze of daffodils. Mom and I had planted a few dozen last fall along the back fence. They had multiplied until now there were too many to count. A lump sprang up in my throat, and tears of pure joy flowed down my cheeks. Suddenly it was spring again . . . and I was home. *It was so good to be home!* I sat down on the back step. Within minutes a gray, furry bundle leaped into my lap. I held her tightly. A rough pink tongue licked at my hand. As I stroked the arched neck, my grin grew wider. My fingers tingled with the vibrations coming from Smokey's body. She was *purring*, and I knew it! I could *feel* my cat purring!

Only minutes later the spell of the warm sun, the flowers, and the feel of the happy silken cat was broken abruptly.

Mom stood before me, her mouth moving quickly, a look half-anguished, half-relieved on her face. Then her brows moved together; her mouth dropped open wide. She clasped one hand over it, and a look of pure horror engulfed her face. I looked up at her questioningly. "What is it? What's the matter, Mom?" She dropped to her knees and held me close. I could feel her sobs, her tears against my cheek and hair. I hugged her. Since I didn't know what was wrong or why she was so upset, it was all I could do.

She stopped at last, then held up one finger, signaling me to wait a minute. She ran into the house and soon was back with pad and pencil. She managed a very small smile.

"Sorry, darling," she had written, "but suddenly you

just disappeared. You frightened us so. We didn't know where you were. We raced through the house, from room to room, calling and calling . . ."

When she had found me, the words had poured out, and it was then, seeing my bewildered face, that she had *remembered*. She'd remembered that I couldn't understand, that I couldn't *hear* her call me *or* her explanation. The realization that it was so easy to forget, that she *wanted* to forget—not really to believe—had thrown her.

After holding her hand for a moment, I arose and announced, "I'm going to feed Smokey, okay? Then maybe read for a while. C'mon, cat, dinnertime. See you later, Mom, I'll be in my room," I was careful to add. She nodded in agreement with a half smile on her face. I marched back into the kitchen. Smokey followed briskly, tail up, sure sign of a happy cat.

After dinner, comfortably squeezed into my old armchair with a well-fed sleeping cat at my side, my feet up on a hassock, I sat thinking. Several new books lay untouched on my desk. There was too much to think about right now. Mom was upset and frightened, really frightened. Dad was, too, I could tell. Dinner had been good, topped by my favorite dessert, a special chocolate cake. A small yellow pad and a pencil had been placed next to the low bowl of daffodils in the center of the table. I had smiled and thanked Mom as I sat down at the pretty table. Coming home *should* be a celebration, and if we weren't gay, at least we were together.

But it had been a quiet dinner. Nobody talked or wrote much—a few nods, smiles, and pointing fingers. We used to talk a lot at dinner. Now you could either

30

eat or write. Doing both was impossible. You had to lay aside your knife and fork, wipe your mouth and fingers, then pick up the pad and pencil. After a couple of questions I just said, "We'll talk after we eat, okay?" It hurt to see them trying so hard to act "normally" when things were so far from normal.

When we'd finished, Mom got up and started to clear the table. I got up to help.

"Let me rinse tonight and you load the dishwasher, Mom," I said.

She shook her head and scribbled: "No, you rest up tonight, darling. You need rest."

I threw the pad down angrily. "No!" I yelled. "I *want* to help! I've been resting for weeks. Nothing's wrong with my hands or arms. Stop treating me like a . . . a damned cripple, will you, please?"

A plate had slipped from my mother's fingers. I watched as it silently shattered into a dozen pieces.

"I'm sorry," I mumbled. "I didn't mean to yell so loud, to startle you so." Mom just nodded.

When we finished cleaning up, I scrubbed out the sink, thinking how strange it was to be glad to be doing a job I'd always tried to get out of before. But working with Mom as I had done hundreds of times before would help us relax, get on with it.

Now I picked up the book with the whirling planets on its cover. With the aid of a wild story about a lush verdant world, much like earth but populated mostly by a handful of telepathic beings, I could stop thinking for a while. I was discovering that there were and always would be retreats, places to go when wounds needed healing, when time, place, even people had to be shut out for a while. Times I would have to stop thinking, guessing, wondering. Times I would just have to get away, even from myself.

Later, after I had climbed into bed and pulled the covers up, I was startled by a thump near my feet, followed by a series of small movements. Reaching down, I gave Smokey's head a last pat. She had come home, too. We'd always shared my bed since she was a kitten. She wouldn't sleep on it while I was away, Mom said. Now we both were back where we belonged, among the things and the people we loved. Safe. Safe at home.

5

■ The next day my mother told me she was taking a leave of absence from school. She had gone back to work seven years ago to teach sixth grade at an inner-city middle school. She loved it, I knew. At first I protested, but she wrote: "Look, Jen, it's going to take awhile to work everything out. We've *all* got a lot to learn and do. You'll have to get to doctors, specialists, the library, shops, to visit friends who don't live nearby, and I'll have to drive you everywhere. Then there's the phone; you need help to make or take a call. Besides all that, I have to check out programs in the schools, talk to people in Special Services and other parents of deaf kids if I can find them and so on. There's so much we don't know yet! So much to find out. I can't do all that and work, too. It just isn't possible!"

Her eyes flashed as she flung the pad at me and dared me to give her an argument. I felt rotten. I hated being somebody who had to be taken care of, who made so much extra work, who kept her from doing what she really wanted to do!

Since I knew it had to be this way right now, though, I shut up for a change and slumped down into my chair, close to tears. When I looked up, I saw my mother rub her forehead as if it were aching, then push a lock of her hair back in place. She reached for the pad wearily and wrote quickly again: "Jenny, I'll go back to teaching in time, but right now I don't intend to put other people's children before my own! You need me now, and I need to be with you. I never considered going back to work full time until you were at least six. I wasn't going to have you and then let someone else bring you up those early important years. We were very lucky, honey, I didn't *have* to work. Lots of mothers do. They have no choice. But Dad was doing pretty well by the time you were born. We'd hoped to have another child. We tried to. It didn't work out that way."

"I always wondered about that."

"Now you know." Mom glanced at her watch. "It's time to exercise. Get out and walk, Jenny."

"Now?"

"Right now!" she said emphatically.

I went.

Donna and Nancy came over after school a couple of times that week and filled me in on what was happening. We kidded around, but there were questions they started to ask, then stopped—crossing out words and changing what they wrote. Both were patient and kind, but I sensed that they were holding back. None of us wanted to tackle the big questions—what happened to me now, what about school and the work I had missed and was missing more of each day? Why hadn't Dan or any of the other kids come over since I got home?

At the end of the week Mom and Dad and I made the trip into New York. Dr. Reese was a sweet, gentle old man. He examined both ears very carefully, shining his bright torch into every spot, searching, searching. Then he led me into a small room, put earphones over my ears, and wrote on my pad: "Tell me by raising your hand if you hear any sound at all."

I sat where he told me to, facing him, a glass partition separating us. He began to move his right hand over a waist-high console, speaking into a microphone held in his other hand. He pushed buttons and turned knobs over and over again. Again and again his lips moved. I didn't raise my hand once. I heard nothing. Nothing at all.

When he'd finished, I looked up at him and asked, "Is there anything you can do to bring any of it back? Anything?"

He shook his head from side to side and took my hand. I couldn't really see it on his mouth, but I knew that he was saying, "No, I'm sorry."

"Would a hearing aid help?" He shook his head and wrote: "No, it only amplifies sound. Helps those who have some hearing."

I knew. I knew, and I'd known all along, even while I denied it to myself, to everyone. This wasn't a dream from which I'd awaken, whole and normal. I wasn't whole anymore. I couldn't hear. I was deaf. I'd be deaf for the rest of my life.

I couldn't cry, not then. I could only look up at him, bewildered and outraged. "You mean I'll never hear a human voice ever again?" I shouted. "How will I learn? How will I live?"

Once more he wrote swiftly: "You'll learn to live with it."

He patted my shoulder and walked out. Others were waiting; he was a very busy man. We left.

Oh, God, why? Why me? Why did this happen to me?

It's so stupid, so senseless. So awful, so wrong! It's not fair! I sat in the car between my parents, screaming inside, silent, numb, just trying to hang on until we got home. Still unbelieving, my blood running cold, fear spreading through every part of me, alone as I had never, ever been before. My father's hands were clenched so tightly on the wheel that his knuckles were white. My mother's eyes searched mine and she held my hands as if she'd never let go, her mouth starting to move and then stopping, remembering no words could reach me now.

Finally, finally, we were home. I sank into a deep chair. Everything erupted then. "Why?" I screamed at Mom and Dad. "Why? Why? *Why?*" I sobbed. "Why me? How can I live in total silence the rest of my life? In a world gone dead! I'll never hear another song again or a laugh or a call, ever, ever again. I'll never be able to understand a movie or TV. I'll never hear a voice, your voices. Ever again!"

The tears ran down my parents' faces. Somehow my father moved, reached for the pad, fumbled with a pen, and wrote: "Jenny, darling, you're so young. In time maybe they'll find a way to help."

"In time? When? In a hundred years? They can transplant kidneys and fix eyes and even sew arms and legs back on sometimes *now!* They can restore faces and operate on hearts and brains now! Why can't they give me back even a little hearing in one ear?! Damn them! Damn them to hell!"

My parents, who had always known what to do or say, sat stunned, mute, helpless. That made it worse.

Stumbling, I ran to my room and wept. I didn't know

where the endless rivers of tears came from; they just went on and on and on. Later, when I was finally able to stop, the release of crying left me exhausted, drained. My eyes hurt, I ached all over, and my head throbbed. I sat there, alive but not sure I wanted to be.

6

■ The next morning I pulled on my oldest jeans and a sweater, washed my face, and headed for the kitchen.

My mother moved to me quickly, her face scanning mine, her expression clearly asking if I was okay.

"I'm all right, I guess," I lied.

Dad kissed me on the cheek. As I ate breakfast, I noticed a message on the yellow pad:

"We've spoken to Dr. Corwin, Jenny. You have a brief appointment with him Friday morning and another with Mrs. Gardner of Greenwich Hospital's Speech and Hearing Dept. for your first lip-reading lesson in the afternoon. She's a teacher of the deaf who has taught for many years, and Dr. Corwin says she's very good. You must learn to lip-read!"

"Can anyone *really* understand by watching people's lips?" I asked them, "How well?"

"*Some* can." My mother wrote quickly. "I spoke to Mrs. Gardner too. She said it's easiest for those who have heard for years to learn."

My father reached for the pad before I could speak and wrote: "You don't have any other option, Jennifer. You must. That's an order!"

"I guess I don't," I told them wearily. Their relief showed clearly on their faces. Mom managed a small smile, which widened as I ate faster.

Well, maybe, I thought, *maybe lip-reading might*

work. I have to understand people somehow. I have to! Because when it came right down to it, most of all, I missed understanding. Hearing means knowing and understanding. Knowing what others thought, questioned, and felt. Knowing people were sad, pleased, joyful, or irritated and angry, and why. I could figure out a little of the way people felt from their faces, even in the way they moved sometimes. But why they were angry or sad, laughing or gay, I couldn't know. The words were gone. The sounds were gone. Inflections, tones, stress, intensity, volume—all the things that conveyed different meaning were gone. Now there were only faces and lips, which moved soundlessly. There was guessing instead of knowing and understanding so little unless someone wrote the words out for me. More and more I was left out.

Maybe I could learn. The knot in my stomach unwound a little. Maybe? I had to.

Mrs. Gardner was something else. A tall, graceful woman with graying hair, she had an oval face and a smile that took away my uneasiness immediately.

When Mom and I walked into the waiting room, she was on her knees before a little boy not more than two years old. Her face glowed as she handed him a red ball on a string.

She rose swiftly as his mother said a few last words to her and led him away. Shyly he looked back at her, grinned, and waved good-bye. He was so young, little more than a baby. But he trusted her, you could tell. From the beginning so did I.

She motioned me to follow her after we had introduced ourselves. I found myself in a small, brightly lit room. One wall contained shelves filled with games and toys.

She waved her hand for me to sit, sat at the table opposite me, and placed a pad and pencil at her right. Looking straight at me, she said, "Talk! Say your name for me." At my puzzled frown, she wrote it all out for me.

I spoke quickly. She smiled, took my hand and placed it so that my fingertips lightly touched my throat, and said, "Again!"

I said my name again and started to ask her why when I discovered that as I spoke, I could feel the vibrations my voice made. Mrs. Gardner explained that I had to use my voice to keep it. If I only mouthed words, then I felt nothing. She'd speak carefully, she told me, and when I didn't understand, she'd repeat, then write. Slowly, very slowly the words began to take shape on her lips, which were narrow and well defined. I caught a word, then a short sentence, then another. It took an awful lot of concentration, but I actually read some words and a sentence or two on her lips before the session was over. When I got tired, I cheated and interrupted. I was curious, too. I wanted to know about the little boy. "Is he deaf?" I asked her.

"Yes, but with the hearing aid, he can hear some sounds," she told me. "He can learn to understand more by reading lips and signs and by practicing using the little bit of hearing he has."

"But he's so little to work so hard . . ."

"The younger we start to work with kids, the better," Mrs. Gardner responded firmly. "It's play for them.

Would you believe I have one who is only eight months old?"

I was surprised and ashamed, too. If a two-year-old could learn this, what had I been so nervous about? She told me that since I already had well-developed language skills, it would be much easier for me, but I had to practice as much as I could with other people. We'd have three hour-long sessions every week from then on, Mrs. Gardner told me.

"How long will it take for me to learn?" I asked anxiously.

"I can't tell you, Jenny. It varies with different people. You'll know as soon as I do," she answered, and that was that.

That night after my first lesson, Mom and I sat down and "talked." Then I had at least another half-hour session with Dad. Each person's mouth was different. I found that out right away. After a couple of weeks I realized Mrs. Gardner was easiest to lip-read, Mom wasn't too hard, but Dad was really rough. At first I couldn't understand a word he said! He spoke too fast, especially when he had an exciting story to tell about his latest client. Dad's a lawyer, and he likes to talk pacing up and down. Often he forgets he's not in court addressing a judge or a jury!

But soon he realized how awful it made me feel to keep saying, "I don't understand. Please say it again." The fourth night it happened, he slumped down into his big chair and scowled at me, scratching his unruly graying hair. It had become a challenge. I wasn't just me anymore. I was a problem to be solved.

"Okay, I'll try to speak slower, Jen. What else would help?"

"Could you turn up the lights so I can see your face easily, please, and tip your head up a little? It's easier if you don't wave your hands so much."

He looked so dead serious and concerned I couldn't resist adding, "Thank goodness you don't have a droopy handlebar mustache like Uncle Harry! If I live to be a hundred, I'll never be able to lip-read *him*. You can't see his upper lip at all!"

The vision of Uncle Harry, plump and with just about all the hair he had in his luxuriant mustache, his pride and joy, cracked us both up. Dad threw back his head and roared until the tears came from his eyes. I felt good watching him. I was glad I had made him laugh. There was no problem understanding when someone was laughing. There was the broad grin, then the open mouth, the shaking shoulders, a hand slapping against a knee or thigh. I was glad that we could still laugh together. Things had been too grim between us lately.

He stopped finally, wiped his eyes, and held out his arms. When I got up, he pulled me to him and hugged me hard.

He held me away and pulled his head back, smiling. Then he pointed his finger at me and said slowly, "Jenny, you are too much!" *And I understood every word!*

7

■ Luckily my dad loved to talk, and as the days passed, we found that gestures helped, too. I didn't know it then, but the pointed finger was the sign for the word "you." Dad had used it instinctively. I began to understand what he said more easily. We used whatever worked for us. Being able to communicate as much as possible, breaking through the barrier of deafness, that was what mattered most. We had taken the first steps; we had made a beginning.

I tried everything to fill up the long days between lessons and the times I saw Donna or Nancy. I helped Mom with dinner and cleaning up. I found that I could do the laundry as well as ever. I just had to put my hand on the machines; the vibrations told me when they started or stopped. The same thing with the dishwasher. I didn't need to hear them; I could *feel* them. That was great.

I walked each morning and late afternoon when the weather was good. Mom made me. At first, it was like walking on a tightrope. Standing still in one place for a long time was uncomfortable, but not bad if I had something to hold onto. I was most comfortable sitting down, but I had to exercise, so since I wasn't the athletic type, walking seemed the best solution. I walked, I gritted my teeth, and I walked.

What bothered me a lot were the strange noises inside

my head, which were with me from the moment I woke up until the moment all thought slid away. Dr. Corwin had told me, when I returned to him after my visit to the specialist in New York, that this was common for people who had *lost* their hearing. Those born deaf didn't feel such sounds.

I began to discover some things that helped distract me from the noises. The best one, the one thing that really worked, was to be terribly involved, to be doing something, anything, that required intense concentration. When I got my hands on a really good book or when I could lip-read someone easily, I completely forgot about the noises. They disappeared for hours at a time. Or maybe *I* disappeared and left them behind. I guess you can get used to practically everything after a while.

Mrs. Gardner taught me finger-spelling, the manual alphabet. It really helped, especially when I got stuck on names or difficult words that looked alike on the mouth.

I tried to teach it to Mom and Dad just as Mrs. Gardner taught it to me. Mom picked it up fast (it's really easy), but Dad muttered and scowled and struggled with it, claiming it was hard to move his fingers into some of the more complicated positions.

"Shake your hand; flex your fingers; then let your fingers hang limp," I told him. "Now wiggle them. Come on, try," I begged. "You *can* do it. You're not old enough to have stiff joints!" Lowered brows and a scowl greeted that remark. "You're not going to cop out on me, are you? Please try, Dad. There are words that are hard to catch. It helps if you spell them out for me. I can figure out the rest better. *Please* . . ."

Mom glared at him and said something. I saw his right eyebrow go up. Then both brows twisted into a deep frown. I knew that look. He was digesting what Mom had said. It wasn't going down too well either. Then he nodded at her.

He sat still for another few seconds, then lifted his right hand. He stared at it as if denying that it belonged to him. The large, gentle, graceful hand that was all thumbs except in a courtroom had betrayed him.

Slowly he let his fingers hang loose and then wiggled them.

"Okay"—the words finally came, slowly—"show me again, Jenny."

Mom and I let go of breaths we hadn't known we were holding. She sat closer to him. I spelled out *A, B, C,* and *D.* "Now do it with me," I said.

He did.

"Again. Now you do it alone."

He did it, then beamed.

I held my breath as he struggled with the *E*, a tough one, the four fingers curled over and just touching the thumb, which extended across the palm.

I demonstrated three or four letters at a time. We repeated those several times before going on, just as Mrs. Gardner had done with me.

We went through the whole alphabet three more times. The last time he got every letter right! I gave him a big smile and flashed index and third fingers up in a *V. V* for victory, *V* for peace! That familiar sign was also the way the letter *V* was finger-spelled. We'd won another battle, and for a moment our worlds converged.

I taught Donna and Nancy how to finger-spell, too.

They both caught on fast. Nancy was terrific at it. She admitted later that she'd found a book in the library which pictured both the manual alphabet and sign language and had been studying and practicing it ever since the night I'd first demonstrated it to her. Behind all that clowning there was a thinker and one of those who followed through. Nancy would learn Sanskrit if it would help. She thought finger-spelling was a piece of cake. It figured.

Mrs. Gardner was thrilled when I told her about what we'd been doing. "That's great, Jenny!" she said, her whole face lighting up. "Keep it up!"

She was very patient, repeating phrases or sentences for me over and over again. Often when I didn't understand and glanced at the pad, she'd shake her head and say, "First, let's try it again." She'd alternate the speed of her speech, too. If it was exaggeratedly slow, I'd lose everything. Slow, deliberate movements were best, but after a while I noticed that she would speed up little by little so that during the last half of the lesson we both were speaking easily and normally most of the time.

I was beginning to feel I was catching on, but easy it wasn't. At one point, after a difficult lesson, I became impatient and complained: "Damn it, learning a completely foreign language is easier! At least you can go home and review the words and sentences in the books. You can listen to the records, too."

"Yes, Jenny, you're probably right, but speech-reading is more important for you now, isn't it?"

"Yeah, I guess so. Okay, of course, it is. I'm sorry, I—"

She held up her hand. "I understand. It is hard. But you're doing remarkably well, honestly, and I'm a better judge of that than you are right now. You know that. Keep practicing, and remember, it does take time."

"Okay, I will."

"Promise?"

"I promise." When she looked at me in that warm but serious way, I would have promised her anything! It mattered to her. She may have said that mostly to encourage me, but she was right. Besides, what choice did I have? I *had* to become really good at lip-reading; it was my ticket home. I didn't know it then, but it was only a partial ticket. The complete ticket would cost a lot more.

I'd just finished feeding Smokey when I felt a hand on my shoulder. I turned to face Mom, whose lips were moving.

"What? Turn a little, Mom. Your face is in shadow. Okay, that's better. What is it?"

"Donna's on the phone, Jen."

"Who?"

"Donna."

"Donna?"

Mom nodded yes. "She wants to know if it's okay to come over." Mom held out the phone to me.

I grabbed it and said, "Sure, sure, Donna, come on over," then handed it back to Mom.

"She'll be over in half an hour," Mom said, putting down the receiver.

"Half an hour?" I repeated to be sure that I had understood. I'd been doing that often lately, to be sure that I'd seen what I thought I saw on someone's lips. "Mom, I'm going to straighten up my room a little. See you later."

She nodded, smiling at my eagerness.

I had just gotten all the books and magazines off my big chair and was putting them on my bookshelf when I felt three hard thumps—vibrations from a stamping foot.

The stamping was a signal I'd asked people to use. If they didn't, I wouldn't know they were in the room until I saw them, and that always startled me so. Donna flung her jacket on my bed, hugged me, and plopped herself into a chair, grinning widely. She was obviously bubbling over with excitement and was rattling away when I stopped her.

"Okay, okay, something's up," I said, "but I can't make out what you're saying. Turn up the light, and take the gum out of your mouth. It's bad for your teeth, and I can't lip-read when you chew! But slow down, please!"

"Okay. Remember, everybody keeps telling us that our country is run by committees, Jen?" Donna said. "The Senate, Congress, business, political parties—practically everything is run by committees."

"Yeah. So?"

"Well, Nancy and I were talking about what had happened to you and how we could help, because this is a rough thing to handle alone, right? You're learning to lip-read, but you can't practice alone. You can practice only with people. With lots of practice you'll learn faster. So anyway, we formed a committee. The Committee for the Return of Jenny Greene to Stevens High."

"Huh? Repeat that last part a little slower, Donna, please."

Donna pushed her hair out of her eyes, repeated, then grabbed the pad and wrote it out for me.

"So," she went on, "each afternoon after school one of us will come over for an hour or two to talk with you, and you can practice with *us*." She grinned, looking very pleased with herself.

"Who? Who's going to come?" I asked, unbelieving.

"We've got it all figured out," Donna said. "Tom takes Monday; I come Tuesday; Larry, Tom's friend, Wednesday; Ellen, Thursday; Nancy, Fridays; and so on. That way you get a chance to be with people and practice lipreading us *and* with Mrs. Gardner and your folks. Maybe you can come to our houses sometimes. Tom drives, so does Ellen; they could pick you up. Nancy and I will see you weekends and other times, too. It's something we *want* to do—so you can come back to school sooner, right? Okay, Jen?"

I looked at Donna, speechless for once. Was it okay? It was incredible, unbelievable! They'd discussed, planned, and offered freely exactly what I needed but couldn't ask for. Even Larry and Ellen, whom I barely knew, had offered to help.

I finally found my tongue. "Donna, that's fabulous! Whose idea was it anyway?"

"Well, Nancy said just practicing with me or her wasn't really enough. We wondered who else we could ask. First we talked about it with Tom. He said he'd been thinking about you since his visit to the hospital. He said you were one of the best writers he had and he needed you!"

"Did he really? Did he say that?" Tom was editor of our school magazine. I'd had a crush on him for ages. Tom, who seemed to hide behind those huge thick glasses but missed nothing, who frowned in class so much that at seventeen he had wrinkles in his forehead! Tom, who didn't hesitate to chew anyone out if one comma was out of place or an article you'd promised wasn't in on time. Tom needed me? Tom wanted to help *me?* Wow!

Holding back the tears, I grabbed Donna's hands and somehow got the words out: "How can I ever thank you?"

"Hush! I told you we all *want* to! Besides, what are friends for? And, Jen . . . not only do we want to do this, but we *need* to do it."

"Need to? Why?"

Donna grabbed the pencil and wrote: "For one thing, because what happened to you could have happened to any of us! We were just lucky we weren't sitting in that seat on the bus. You're bright, Jenny. You've always picked up things fast. But you can't learn this all by yourself, and we think this is something only *we* can do. You've got to let us try!"

"Who's stopping you?" I asked, grinning, half ready to cry again.

"It's all settled then. Hey, it's late! Gotta go. See you soon. Take care."

With a quick hug and a wave she was gone.

I rushed into the kitchen to tell Mom, who grinned at me as she wiped her hands and said calmly, "Yes, I know, love. Nancy called yesterday to ask me if I thought it was all right. Bless them!" We hugged each other hard, thrilled.

Mom looked tired. Housework wasn't her thing, I knew. She hated it and hated staying home.

"You miss school a lot, don't you?" I asked.

She nodded, poured a cup of coffee, and waved me to the table.

"The Committee for the Return of Jenny Greene. I like that, Jen," Mom said. "That is undoubtedly very advanced planning on their part. Marvelous of them. They'll see it through, too, I think."

"I do, too. But, Mom, is is it possible? Will I be allowed to go back to school—to a regular school?"

"Yes, love. There's a special law, passed several years ago. I found out about it while you were in the hospital. Schools are required to take"—she paused and swallowed—"*handicapped* students and provide special programs for them. You can attend a mainstreamed program in the regular public high schools. We'll investigate further, but if you want it and feel you can handle it, they'll take you. Dad has sent to Washington for a copy of the law and will check it over thoroughly. We need to know exactly what it requires the schools to provide; all the details."

"Mom, will there be others? Others deaf like me?"

"Yes, there'll be other hearing-impaired youngsters. I don't know how many, but there will be others, some hard-of-hearing, some deaf, I'm sure of that."

"That's good. I'd hate to be the only one."

Hearing-impaired? What did that mean? I wondered. I couldn't hear, period. I was deaf. It must mean kids who didn't have normal hearing but heard. They'd wear hearing aids to help.

Mom touched my arm. "Jenny, it's late and you haven't exercised yet. Get going!" she ordered.

"Do I have to? I wanted to finish—" She glared at me icily. My mother can turn into the Wicked Witch of the West in nothing flat. I went.

I hadn't walked for more than ten minutes when I noticed the sky beginning to darken. It was early to be so dark. Suddenly the sun was completely gone. I turned back. As the first drops fell, I ran, glad that I had thrown on a light jacket. A huge jagged white slash brightened the sky ahead of me. Then there was another —as though an unseen angry painter, not satisfied with his work, were slashing the sky with an outsized brush.

It was several seconds before I realized that I wasn't frightened. There had been no crash or roar. The slashes were lightning, followed by thunder probably—but not for me. Only bright flashes of light against a darkening sky now for me. I ran harder, heading for home.

After dinner I told Dad about the committee. He sipped his coffee and carefully said, "That's great! I've got news, too." Smiling broadly, he said, "Jenny, you'll be able to start driving lessons in July, as we planned."

My eyebrows rose in surprise. "I will? They'll let me drive a car?"

He paused dramatically. "Deaf people drive," he finally wrote. "There was a deaf guy at the clerk's office this morning paying a fine for a minor violation. I checked with the court clerks and the Motor Vehicle Department, too. Since driving is 99 percent dependent on vision, the state doesn't question your right to drive a car. Statistics show that deaf people are very good drivers! There *is* a minor problem. I called a couple of the local driving schools and got a very cold reception. They won't teach you. Claim they don't know how, the idiots!"

"Oh, no!"

"Not to worry, I'll teach you myself. It's really not that hard. We'll talk each step over, you'll read the manual carefully, and we'll go up to the northern part of town and practice a lot on the back roads. Bill, a guy I work with, has a deaf cousin. He says an extra-wide rearview mirror is a good idea, so we'll get one of those for you."

"Oh, Dad, that's great! I didn't know—I didn't dare even let myself think about it. Won't it take a lot of time?"

His eyes narrowed, and he glared at me. "Whatever time it takes, it takes," he said. "Jennifer, you want to learn, don't you?"

"Oh, yes! I hate always having other people drive me everywhere. All my friends can drive or are taking lessons. Now I can too! Oh, Dad!" I jumped up and hugged him hard.

We talked for a while, but I was too excited to concentrate. There was a special on TV I knew they both wanted to watch, so I went to my room. I had tried to lip-read TV a couple of times. I couldn't. I told myself it didn't matter. I didn't always believe me.

I put my book down and stroked Smokey behind her ears.

"Wanna play?" I asked her. She lifted her head for a second, licked my hand, then dropped her head down between her paws, pulling her tail past her chin and conking out.

"You ate too much," I told her. As I stroked her, my thoughts returned to the afternoon's conversation with Mom. The special programs for the handicapped—and Mom's face as she tried not to stumble over that word. Handicapped. Her protests about not working for a while. How long was a "while"? She missed her work more than she let on. She'd always had stories to tell about "her kids." Sometimes I was jealous. After all, she was *my* mother. Now I needed her, and I didn't *want* to need her—not this way, to help me so much. I hated needing help to call my friends. I mean, there were things you just couldn't *say* with her standing there. It wasn't a *real* phone conversation; just simple questions and answers had to do. You just didn't have any privacy using the phone that way. Having anyone help me with the phone was a real drag. But it was either do it that way or not be able to make or take calls at all. That was worse.

Finally, I turned the lights out and snuggled under the covers, Smokey curled up at my feet.

It was very late but I couldn't sleep. This had happened before. Many nights I had trouble falling asleep. I figured I was overexcited. So many ideas, questions, and thoughts crowded my mind.

Would the committee plan work? Would my friends and classmates really come? Would it really help? Would anything help? I tossed and turned for a long time before I fell asleep.

8

■ They came. All of them came. Day after day, week after week, each schoolday afternoon, they came. On beautiful, sunny days, they came. On windy, rain-splashed, chilly days, they came. The lilacs faded, forsythia greened and gave way to regal stalks of iris. Later stubborn wild daisies pushed their way to the sun. Still, they came.

I learned more than lip-reading that spring. I couldn't go to school, so my classmates brought a special sort of school to me. I could look forward to being with someone at least part of the day to share jokes and stories or just to kid around. Donna or Nancy usually came on weekends, too. Sometimes we'd go shopping or visit the museum and nature center.

With Tom, I was kind of shy at first. He was such a big wheel at school. I figured a question or two might help, and having noticed the stack of books piled in the front seat of his old, beat-up car, I blurted, "Have you read them all?"

Tom grinned and settled back comfortably in Dad's big leather chair. "Nope. Most of them, though. Has Dan stopped by? He said he might."

"No, he hasn't." I'd been wondering why Dan hadn't come. I'd thought he liked me. He'd asked me to the dance even if it had been at the last minute.

"Probably busy," Tom said too quickly. "If he doesn't hit the books, he'll flunk American History for sure, maybe algebra, too."

"I guess so," I said. "Maybe . . . maybe he feels funny about coming over. Some people do. Like . . . like I'm contagious or something!"

Tom didn't answer right away. Then, speaking very carefully, he said, "Could be. Jenny, most people have never met a deaf person. Anyone different scares some creeps! Some people have no guts!"

"Oh, Tom, c'mon. It doesn't matter that much!" I lied.

Tom put on his haughty-professor face and hit back. "It *does* matter. There are certain things that do matter, Jenny—to me anyway."

"Like what?"

Tom said firmly, "Being honest. Telling it like it is. That matters. I'm going to spend my life doing that."

"Oh?"

"Sure." Tom's eyes glistened behind the thick glasses. "Going to major in journalism when I start college next fall."

Tom enjoyed sounding off, about the stupidity of exams, about dumb rules, about all kinds of things. I asked him to repeat a few words, which he did. He and the others would always repeat or change the phrasing when I had trouble following. They all were so patient.

Tom had brought me a couple of booklists. "So you can keep up," he explained. "Mr. Stein asked me to give you this one," he said, "and this one I made up for you. The ones on both lists you *must* read."

Patient, yes, and still as bossy as ever!

"Okay, will do," I said, glancing at the piles of books all over the room.

Too soon he had to leave, taking his dream with him. He knew where he was going. I wished I did. I wished I could work again in the noisy, cluttered room at school we called our office. I missed helping put the magazine together. I thought of the ancient typewriter whose *e* was always sticking, of Tom and some of the others sneaking a smoke and jamming the ashtray into a desk drawer if we saw a teacher coming, hysterical calls to the printers, kidding around afterward when the work was done. It was so much easier talking to and getting to know people, especially boys, when you worked together.

Ellen, whom I'd barely said hello to at school, never missed her day. It was Ellen who told me about Billy, the new boy from Florida whom so many of the girls flipped over. When Ellen imitated stuck-up Sally trying to get his attention and being snubbed, I laughed so hard I almost cried. Shy, quiet Ellen didn't miss much. It wasn't easy to get used to Ellen's speech, but it became easier as time went on.

One day late in May Ellen ran in much later than I'd expected her.

"Sorry, Jen!" she said, breathing hard. "My sister Meg got home from college last night, and we were up gabbing for hours. I overslept, cut most of my classes, but I just had to get over to tell you!"

"Tell me what?" I asked.

"Well, I told Meg about you and our group and how

hard you're working at learning lip-reading, and she told me about one of her best friends at school, Kathy Benton!"

"Who?"

"Kathy Benton," Ellen finger-spelled for me. "Kathy's parents are both deaf. Her father is a chemist at National Pharmaceuticals. Her younger brother, Joe, is deaf, too. He's a senior at Stevens High!"

Seeing my puzzled look, Ellen quickly picked up the nearby pad and wrote out the last sentences.

"Oh? What else did Meg say?" I asked.

Ellen leaned forward and spoke slowly and carefully. "She said Joe's a real great guy, bright and not shy at all. He loves to talk with people! Kathy was very interested in you. She said she'd tell Joe all about you, and she was sure he'd get in touch with you as soon as he could!"

"Oh, Ellen, do you really think he will?"

"Sure, why not? His parents are really into working for deaf people, Kathy said. She often acts as interpreter for them because their speech is hard to understand." Ellen paused, then asked, "Have you been in touch with any other deaf people, Jen?"

"No. It's odd. We know there must be others, but nobody seems to know anyone. Maybe because you can't tell that someone's deaf just by looking at them. We look just like everybody else!"

"I never really thought about it that way," Ellen said. "Does it make you feel funny sometimes? It must be harder on you than you let on, Jenny."

I didn't like the look on her face, even though I knew that with Ellen it meant more concern than pity. I noticed I was getting awfully touchy about the slightest hint of pity from anyone. It really bugged me.

Later, long after Ellen had gone, I thought about how people reacted to me now. They didn't stare at me. It was as if I'd suddenly become invisible, as if because I had ears, then obviously I must hear. When I told people I couldn't, they often didn't believe me! I didn't look different, but I was. Would I ever get used to it? I had to. Mrs. Gardner, Dr. Corwin, everyone said it would take time. But how long? I wondered. How long?

9

■ My sessions with Mrs. Gardner went smoothly now. Each week I understood more. The day arrived when she said what I'd been longing to hear. It was a nasty, rainy day, but the little room brightened as she sat solemnly across from me, smiled warmly, and said, "Jenny, you're a natural! You haven't missed more than a phrase or a word or two in the past three sessions!"

"I do understand you almost all the time now, don't I?" I answered. "I don't even really think about it. I just do it!"

"Indeed you do! Jenny, I've taught lip-reading for more than fifteen years. I've had only two other students who learned as quickly."

The brilliant smile she gave me made me feel almost as good as her words. "But you have to keep at it. The one-to-one relationship is easiest; it always will be. Lip-reading in a group is harder, but you'll get used to it."

"I guess so, Mrs. Gardner. Do you know of any other deaf people around my age? I'd like to meet others like me."

Mrs. Gardner frowned, her face concerned. "No, Jenny, I'm sorry, I don't. We get mostly older people with hearing problems here at the clinic," she answered. "But I'll ask around and get in touch with you if I hear of someone, I promise. Meanwhile, you keep trying to lip-read everyone you can, everywhere. Try not to be discouraged if some people are difficult."

"I know. Thanks, Mrs. Gardner. You made it easy. I forgot to be scared by the end of our first lesson! You know, the people I feel most comfortable with are the ones I lip-read best. The first few minutes with anyone new are tough. There are always those big questions. Will I be able to do it? Will they let me try? Not everybody does. Lots of people are upset as soon as I say I'm deaf."

Mrs. Gardner looked at me searchingly. "Is that all you tell them?"

"No. I also ask them to talk a little slower than usual and tell them I'll try to lip-read what they are saying."

"Good girl! That's the best way to handle it."

"Everyone says, 'Oh, I'm sorry,' so then I say, 'Don't be. Just let me try. If I can't, then please write on this pad.' "

"Fine!"

"Know something? It's wild! Those I can understand think I'm a cockeyed wonder. Those I can't think I can't lip-read at all! The whole world has become evenly divided into one of three groups: those I can understand right away easily, those I can understand after getting used to their lips and speech patterns, and, finally, those who I can't make it with at all!" I paused. "That leaves an awful lot of people I'll never be able to understand, doesn't it?"

"Maybe," she said reluctantly. "But stay with it, Jenny, and have a wonderful summer!"

"You, too," I said, and left quickly. I hate good-byes. I knew I'd miss our lessons.

Nancy arrived early, carrying a bunch of the season's first wild daisies. "Hi, Nancy, good to see you. Since you're here, it must be Friday."

Nancy giggled. "Hi, nut! Of course it's Friday!"

"With no school, sometimes I lose track."

"When you get back, you'll miss the free time, lazybones. Here, aren't they pretty?" she asked, thrusting the daisies at me.

"Gorgeous! One sec while I put them in water."

"I'm gonna spend hours with that Holler-head Thatcher tonight," Nancy said when I returned.

"Who?" I asked, puzzled.

Nancy spelled out the name, and I laughed.

"Having to baby-sit with that little creep is sweat. That five-year-old kid has a mouth on him you wouldn't believe! And quiet games this kid doesn't know from!"

I smiled. Trust Nancy to play the whole bit for a laugh and to put the job down subtly so I'd forget it had been ages since I had had a job sitting. Who'd use a sitter who couldn't hear a kid cry or call for help in an emergency? Or even understand whatever he's saying half the time. Little kids are rough to lip-read!

"Hey!" Nancy waved to get my full attention. "Did you get all that, Jen?" I nodded. "Gee, you understand me really well now," she said, happy about it. "How's it going with the others?"

"Let's see. Tom, I can lip-read most of the time, and he's patient when I can't. Donna, when she doesn't talk too fast, is real easy. You and she are the easiest because

I see you most often. It took weeks to catch on to Ellen. I still make mistakes with her, so we finger-spell and write a lot. Larry is hard; he doesn't open his mouth much. He said last week he was sorry, but he could come only once more. He's got a job at the golf course. He starts right after school lets out next week. Said he was real lucky to get it. His uncle knows the pro."

"And how! All the guys want those jobs. I wish I knew what I'll be able to get this summer. I wanted to try for a counselor's job—doesn't pay much, but it's fun. Mom said to try, but you know, she's been—well, funny lately."

"What do you mean funny?"

"Don't know—can't put my finger on it, but I have a hunch something's wrong. Jen, I came home the other day, and Mom looked lousy. Her eyes were all puffy, like she'd been crying. She's been awfully sharp and short-tempered with me and Davy lately. Nothing we do is right, and she's never been like that; you know that, Jenny."

"Everybody blows up once in a while," I said weakly.

"Yeah, sure, but well, Dad's not home much these days, even less than usual. And late last Sunday, just before he left for Boston, I heard them screaming at each other. Then I heard a crash like somebody broke something heavy. I started to go downstairs and see what was going on when I heard the door slam real hard and a car drive off. When I got down, no one was there, and Mom wasn't in her bedroom either. The bathroom door was locked, and water was running hard."

I looked at Nancy, and I could tell we both were thinking the same thing. Hard-running water is loud—it blots out other sounds. Like someone sobbing. Like when you need to let go and you don't want anyone to hear . . .

Then suddenly Nancy bit her lips, screwed up her face, and covered it with her hands. The tears ran down her cheeks. She was crying and saying something; but her lips were covered, and I couldn't understand a word. I jumped up and put my arms around her and said, "Oh, Nancy! Nancy, honey."

She was trying to tell me something, but realizing she couldn't, she cried even harder. I stood there, holding her for a while, and then ran to get some tissues.

When she finally stopped shaking, I pushed them into her hands and got down on my knees as she struggled for control.

"It . . . it can't be that bad, Nancy," I said.

"Jenny, Mom said last night that she, Davy, and I were going up to stay with Grandpa and Grandma Whalen for the summer, maybe longer. Their farm is hundreds of miles away, up past Albany. We rented our house when Dad was transferred here four years ago, and now it looks like we may be leaving for good. We leave next week. Mom says there are a hundred things to do. I have to help."

"You've all always gone there for a few weeks every summer," I reminded her. "Maybe she just wants to stay longer this year?"

"Mom said she wants to go *home*. That Grandma needs us, but, Jenny, I think . . . I think Mom and Dad are breaking up. I'll have to leave you, school, all my friends. I could kill them! What's the matter with people anyway?" Nancy grabbed my hands. "I'll miss you so."

"I'll miss you too! Oh, Nancy, you'll write, won't you?"

"Sure, sure, we'll both write! Long letters! And try to visit. We can work something out."

"Sure! Now don't cry anymore," I pleaded, seeing the tears spring from her eyes again. "Look, it's not Siberia. It's not the end of the world!"

It might as well have been. We both knew that. And I couldn't think of anything to say before I hugged her again and closed the door behind her. Nancy hadn't even hinted at anything's being wrong. I guessed she hadn't wanted to worry me. Damn! And now she was gone from my life. It was too much. I jumped up, ran to my room, threw myself on the bed, and cried, feeling totally frustrated, helpless, and angry. My friend was in trouble, and I couldn't do a thing. I wanted to scream at Nancy's parents, but Mom came in just then, so I screamed at her.

"Don't they know what they're doing to Nancy and Davy?" I yelled.

Mom flinched and lowered her hand, a signal for me to lower my voice. "Exactly what's wrong, Jen?" Mom asked. When I told her, she sadly but calmly took both my hands in hers, then spoke carefully. "People change, Jenny. Sometimes married people grow in different directions; these things happen. Often everyone is better off in the end than staying together unhappily. Of course, a breakup hurts." She paused for several seconds. "Honey, are you crying for Nancy or yourself?"

My mother has an uncanny way of asking a pointed question that forces me to think beyond the obvious. "Both of us, I guess," I admitted. "We're losing each other because they're too . . . too stupid to get along. It's not fair!"

"No, it's not. It's not a fair world. I'm so sorry, honey."

"I'm sorry I screamed at you, Mom."

"I know."

"I still think it stinks!"

"Yes, it does," Mom agreed. "Jen, could you come and help me unpack the groceries? I bought much more than I intended to and it's late."

"Sure." I got up quickly, glad to move, to have something to do. I'm not all that crazy about chores, who is? And I had a hunch Mom didn't really need my help all that much, but on the other hand . . .

10

■ There were a dozen cars and a couple of motorbikes in Ellen's driveway as Donna, Nancy, and I pulled up.

"Hey," I said, "you said this was going to be a small farewell party for Nancy? It looks like it's a great big bash!"

"Beats me." Donna shrugged, unbuckling her seat belt.

Nancy said, "The committee and some of their friends. Maybe friends brought friends. Who knows? C'mon, Jenny, it'll be fun!"

Donna tapped my shoulder. "They're nice people! C'mon, let's go!"

Mrs. Halpern, Ellen's mother, greeted us and led us downstairs to the huge paneled playroom. The room was packed. Several couples were dancing. Others were standing around or flung onto sofas or chairs or were squatting cross-legged on the floor. My eyes swept the room, searching for a familiar face. From the farthest corner I saw a waving arm and recognized Ellen. She started to get up, but someone pulled her back down. She grinned at me, shrugged her shoulders, and put up her hand showing two spread fingers. I waved back; she meant two minutes.

A hand touched mine, and I turned to face Tom, who had a very pretty girl at his side.

"Hi, Jenny! Good to see you!" he said carefully.

"This is Jane Tompkins."

"Hi! Glad to meet you," I said.

Tom looked around, then took my hand and led me to a chair near the window, where he parked himself and Jane at my feet.

"How are you doing, Jen?" he asked.

"Okay, I guess. I never expected so many people!"

"The word gets out fast, doesn't it? Like some punch?" he asked and, without waiting for answer, went to get it.

Jane smiled and said something very quickly.

"Sorry I didn't catch that," I told her. "I'm . . . I'm deaf. Would you repeat it, please?"

Her eyebrows rose. "Oh, I'm sorry!" she said. "I didn't know!"

"Don't be, just talk slower, so I can lip-read you. Okay?"

"Sure. You mean you can't hear anything?" Her hands went to her face, and her mouth dropped open for several seconds. "How awful! How? I mean, were you born that way?"

"No. I lost my hearing in an accident. I fractured my skull." The dismay on her face gave way to something else: pity. She pitied me. It stung.

Before I could say anything to wipe that look off her face, a tall, lanky boy joined us and spoke swiftly to Jane. His face was turned away from me. I twisted my head and tried to see his mouth. I couldn't. Jane grinned, spoke quickly to him, and then turned to me.

"Uh, excuse me, Jenny. See you later, okay?" she said, and they hurried away.

I turned toward the group of kids nearest me, trying to make out what they were talking about. I caught a phrase once but lost track right away. I didn't know where to look. There was no way of figuring who would speak next. By the time I saw someone's mouth move the words were gone.

My eyes roamed over the room, searching for someone I knew. I spotted Larry and another guy halfway across the room. Grim and determined, I walked over to them.

"Hi, Larry. How've you been?" I asked

He looked surprised, but he recovered quickly, smiled, and said, "Hey, Jenny! Great to see you! How's everything going? This is Fred."

I caught most of it. "Hi. Okay," I answered. "I'm studying hard and . . . and keeping busy. I miss school, though."

Both of them laughed, and Larry muttered something I couldn't catch.

"Uh—say that again, please."

Larry took a deep breath, then said slowly, "You've got to be kidding!"

"No. No, I'm not," I began. "I really do miss—" both boys turned their faces abruptly away, Fred elbowing his companion in the ribs. I saw their mouths drop open and moved forward to see what had caught their attention.

It wasn't a what. It was who. A tanned freckled-faced blond guy in tight white chinos and a navy blue shirt stood there ramrod straight, yet at ease, his arms stretched wide and high as if greeting everyone at once. Somebody's older brother maybe? He made all the other guys look like kids somehow, even though he was shorter than several of them. Wow! I didn't think anybody real could look like that! An empty chair appeared miraculously, and within seconds everyone in the room was sprawled around him. His mouth widened in a big grin. Then his lips moved quickly, and they all laughed. Someone else spoke; he answered. More laughing. His face turned solemn, and he spoke again, longer this time. Every eye was glued to his face. They cared about what he was saying. I understood that much, but that was all. The star of this show had arrived and had taken over, but someone had turned off the audio! Who was he? What was happening? What was he saying? What were the others asking or replying? Why was everyone suddenly so serious, so excited? A heated discussion went on and on, but it was impossible to understand, even to guess at.

My heart sank. The noises inside my head got louder. I clenched my lips to keep from screaming. I circled behind everyone and crept up close to Donna, whispering urgently, "What's he saying? Tell me!"

She faced me for a second and said, "He's talking about the draft protests. Later! Hush!"

I didn't dare ask who he was. Later never came. I couldn't ask anything or say anything more. I sat there silent, empty, apart. Alone, left out.

It was torture, and nobody even knew. They had forgotten. They all had forgotten so easily. I didn't belong anymore. And there was nothing I could do about it. Nothing.

I moved away from the group, hoping no one would

notice. I had to get away. Mrs. Halpern was standing in the doorway, listening, watching.

"Please . . ."

I waved her into the small adjoining room. Desperately I squeezed the tears back as she looked at me, concerned. "Please call my folks. I want to go home!"

She gasped, put her hands on my shoulders, and asked, "Are you all right, Jenny?"

"Yes . . . no! Please. I can't take anymore."

She winced, reached for the wall phone, and dialed quickly, taking my hand as we waited. I caught a few words on her lips "Alice, for God's sake! Come and take your daughter home!"

I mumbled my thanks and ran upstairs to the front door. Away. Away from what I saw on her face, away from everyone, away from all I had missed and longed for. I ran down the long driveway, praying Mom would come soon.

As soon as I got in the car, Mom flicked the ceiling light on and faced me.

"That bad, Jenny?" she asked.

"Worse!" I said. "I couldn't understand *anything* after the first few minutes, Mom. I can't lip-read what I can't see! Lip-reading works only *some* of the time. In a setup like that it doesn't work at all! I'm never, ever going to be with people like I used to. I . . . I can't!"

My mother struggled to say something. She couldn't find the words. There weren't any.

Not daring to let myself think, I read for hours that evening. Finally, I went to bed. I tried to sleep. I couldn't. The human brain is screwy. At least mine is. Sometimes I owned it; sometimes it owned me. Now thoughts came and went. Questions popped into my head. I remembered things I didn't want to remember. I couldn't turn it off. Pictures of Nancy clowning, teasing, crying slid through my mind. No more Nancy to urge me on, to make me laugh, to count on. Why did I have to lose her, too? Why *now* of all times?

There were so many things I didn't know. Not knowing, that's what was so hard. What could I do? What could I ever *be?* Could I really learn to manage in a group of people? Even a small one? Would others accept me? Would I be an outsider forever?

I thought of Dan, of Tom, of the boy at the party who had made my heart beat faster. Would *any* boy ever want a deaf girl? Why would any boy want a girl you couldn't take to the movies or even watch TV with? Or call or talk to or joke with easily? Would *anyone* want me? Ever?

Finally, I cried like a baby until there were no tears left. I felt cold and empty—empty as I had never ever been before. I was beyond rage, beyond tears. Beyond hope? Maybe that, too. My eyes and my head ached. I dragged myself into the bathroom, washed my face, reached for the aspirin in the medicine cabinet. I took two and stared at the bottle in my hand. It was a large one, the giant economy size Mom always buys. Two hundred tablets.

The bottle was almost full. How many would it take? How many would I have to swallow to sleep and not ever wake up again? To leave it all behind forever . . . the ceaseless noises in my head, the laughing, talking faces I couldn't understand, the people who didn't know me anymore, didn't see me anymore, the endless struggling to understand, the helplessness, the bluffing, the pretending that so much didn't matter, to others, to myself. It would be so easy. A hundred tablets? More? The whole bottle? Could I drink enough to get them all down? Was there an easier way?

I put the bottle down and glanced into the cabinet again. A stack of razor blades rested on the top shelf. Brand-new. Two inches of thin cold steel wrapped in paper. Ten of them. I'd need only one. A quick slash across each wrist in the right place. Easy. My arms are as skinny as the rest of me, and I have "good" veins. The nurses had told me that. But how deep did you have to cut? How long would it take? I held out my left arm, the blade in my right hand. I touched it to my wrist. Cold against my skin. But for only a few seconds —then no more cold, no more heat, no more anything.

It would hurt. Much? How much? How long? Dear God! I don't want to hurt anymore! Suddenly the bathroom door swung open. I jumped back, startled. Who was there? No one! A tip of furry tail touched my ankle. Smokey! Oh, Smokey! With a graceful leap, she jumped up on the counter and rubbed against my arm. The blade fell from my hand as I instinctively reached out to stroke her. She purred as I scratched her throat. I grabbed her up in my arms and hugged her close, buried my face in her neck. I shook all over.

When I stopped trembling at last, I let her go. Carefully I put the aspirin and all the blades back on the shelf.

11

■ Suddenly the world shrank. School was over. Nancy had left for her grandparents' farm. Tom and Larry both were working. Each stopped by for only a few minutes once or twice over the summer.

The first week in July Ellen told me her father had been transferred to Chicago. They were leaving at the end of the month. We promised faithfully to write to each other.

Donna had gotten a job as a waitress, and we got together when she was free; but she had to work lots of weekends and had only one day off. She was often so tired then that I didn't press her to stay, even though I longed to be with her.

I began to realize that it wasn't sound I missed most. It was *people*. It was contact with other kids. My friends . . .

A plague that only I was aware of seemed to have descended on our town. Except for Donna, moving, vacations, and transfers had wiped out the over-six, under-twenty population of the neighborhood, which now consisted of one person. *Me*. With Mom's help, I tried to call some of the kids in other neighborhoods I didn't know very well. No one answered, or they were away, or they were busy.

I worked in the garden. I tried to sketch with the

colored pencils Nancy had brought to the hospital. I tried oil paints and working with clay, too. No fun. I was lousy at both.

If I had been an eager reader before, I was now an addict. I was going through four or five books a week. A book a day to keep the demons away.

The librarians at our small local branch were super. They always had extra time to chat for a few minutes, to suggest a new book. Mrs. Flynn, knowing I was big on cats, led me to Paul Gallico's books. Miss Evans introduced me to the unforgettable letters of Anne Sullivan Macy. Sullivan, who was only twenty years old when she accepted the challenge of trying to break through to Helen Keller, really grabbed me. My awe increased as her letters revealed her fears and doubts, her endless experiments, the vision she clung to.

I wrote long letters to Nancy and Ellen and waited anxiously for the mail each day. By mid-July I had the neatest, most organized room in our house and the best-groomed cat in town.

By August I was climbing the walls. I thought often of Ellen's sister's friend and the deaf boy she told me about. Where was he? Had she forgotten? I wondered. Why hadn't I heard from him? Or from Mrs. Gardner? I missed our lessons more than I ever thought I would.

One cool morning, just after my sixteenth birthday, Mom and I went down to the Motor Vehicle Department, and I got my learner's permit. Dad's promised lessons would begin that Saturday. Something at last to look forward to. I studied the drivers' manual carefully, wondering how my father could instruct me while I was behind the wheel. I could lip-read when someone else was driving, but if *I* was behind the wheel . . . no way!

That night before our first lesson Dad presented me with a book, *Talk with Your Hands.*

"But how are we supposed to learn sign language in one night?" I protested.

He scowled at me, shaking his head. "Dope!" he said. "We have to learn only a handful of signs: stop, go, drive, turn left, right, slow down, maybe a few more. It's easy!"

"C'mon, you had trouble with the manual alphabet! How come you figure this is so easy?"

"Jennifer, you can be so stubborn! Come here. Sit down next to me," he commanded.

I did, still skeptical.

He put both hands up, fingers curled, and made a circular motion, as though he were driving. "What does that mean to you, Jenny?" he demanded.

"Driving. You're pantomiming driving a car," I replied.

"Right! And that, young lady, is the sign for 'drive' and 'car,' too. You can see it at a glance out of the corner of your eye and understand quickly. Right?"

He was right.

"Now, this means 'stop.'" He put his left palm out and brought the side of his hand down upon it quickly in a chopping movement. I copied it. It was easy!

"You're brilliant, absolutely brilliant!" I yelled.

"Sometimes," he acknowledged with a broad grin. My father is a very modest man. Sometimes.

We also made up a set of touch signals. A hand on

my knee meant "much slower." A finger lightly touching my upper cheekbone meant "Look in your rearview mirror," a tap on my shoulder meant "Check the left lane," and so on.

The first time I drove alone, a million butterflies invaded my stomach. I managed, with effort, to hit twenty miles an hour. My foot pressed the accelerator so gingerly that it took forever to go a few blocks. After a few weeks and lots of short trips the butterflies found a home somewhere else.

Once they'd left and I was comfortable behind the wheel, I made longer trips—to Donna's house, the library, shops, even tag sales and flea markets once in a while. Wheels opened up the world again. When driving, I was in control. I was able to do what all the other kids my age did. When driving, I was just like everybody else.

On one of Donna's days off, she and I drove to a giant outdoor antique and flea market about a half hour away from home. It was wild. Row after row of stuff was loaded onto the backs of station wagons, stacked on long metal tables, peeking out of boxes, cartons, and trunks. Some things were even spread out on blankets or cloths on the ground.

"Wow! How will we find any of that old blue-and-white pottery my mother collects here?" Donna asked, gasping. "There's so much!"

"We can try!" I answered. "It'd make a real jazzy gift for her birthday. C'mon, let's look close! I'll bet we'll find something."

It was a real treasure hunt. We ignored the junk and

most of the paintings, prints, old tools, glass of every color, furniture, and the rest. The old dolls and toys and books were harder to passs by; we couldn't help lingering over them.

One dealer had a bunch of old toys; mechanicals, he called them. They moved when you wound them up with a key—jumping, saluting, waving their arms, or even running! We dragged ourselves away from them (after one quick look at the price tags).

Finally, we found a plate and a small pitcher of Flow Blue china. I looked at it closely as Donna explained to the dealer that we wanted it but couldn't afford it. She turned to me and said, "She'll take five dollars less. What do you think, Jenny? That's still more than I wanted to spend."

"It's pretty, but there's a big chip underneath, look!" I handed the pitcher back to the dealer. She and Donna examined it. Then reluctantly the dealer sighed and lowered the price again. Donna bought it, grinning at me as she paid for it. The chip wouldn't show when the pitcher was placed on a shelf.

We wandered on past the beer cans, the postcards, the china, the silver, and the bottles. The things people collect you wouldn't believe! We stopped for sodas, bought a string of colored beads and a tiny china kitten for ourselves, then headed for the car. The sun was going down.

Donna had driven earlier so that I could lip-read her. Now it was my turn. Most of the time I drove during the daylight hours. We got on the parkway and were about halfway home when the last rays of light vanished and darkness descended. We couldn't talk to each other in the dark. I could ask a question, and Donna would nod her head yes or no. That was it.

I concentrated on driving. It was getting harder to see, and I was a little uncomfortable. Familiar landmarks had disappeared; the lights seemed fewer and farther apart. Traffic was light, so there weren't many red rear lights on cars in front of me to guide me.

I drove steadily and carefully as I always do, noticing cars often swinging into the left-hand lane and passing me. If they were in such a big hurry, so what, let them pass me. I didn't like driving too fast.

Unexpectedly I felt a hand press my knee lightly. Glancing right briefly, I saw Donna gesturing and talking.

Annoyed, I said, "Donna, cut it out! You know I can't understand you when I'm driving!"

Her hand tapped again, then waved to the right, then repeated the motion. What on earth did she want? I wondered. What was she trying to tell me? She knew I couldn't understand, and I couldn't stop right in the middle of the parkway! What was wrong? I quickly checked my lights, then glanced in the rearview mirror. Nothing. "Donna! Please stop it! I can't—" Before I could finish, the words stuck in my throat as I caught sight of the flashing lights of the patrol car on my left, barely a foot away and moving closer, cutting me off, forcing me to the right.

Oh, God, what had I done?! I pulled over as far right as I could and stopped. A furious state trooper was out of the car in seconds and motioning for me to roll down the window. Boy, was he mad!

I gulped and put up my hand, trying to halt the stream of angry words. "Officer, wait a minute, please. I didn't hear your siren. I can't, I'm deaf. Just tell me what I've done wrong, please, and my friend will interpret if I don't understand you."

His mouth dropped open, and the scowl disappeared. I switched on the inside light as he said, "Okay. I've been following you for miles! Do you realize you've been doing twenty-five miles an hour in a forty-mile-an-hour minimum zone, young lady? Get off at the next exit and wait for me!"

"Oh, I'm sorry!" I followed his directions and pulled into the deserted gas station right off the exit. Seconds later the trooper was at my side.

"This parkway has a forty-mile-an-hour minimum speed limit," he said. "You *must* do forty at least. Driving so slowly could endanger other drivers. I have to give you a ticket. Your license and registration, please."

"I'm sorry," I told him as I reached into the glove compartment. "I didn't realize I was going *that* slowly. I figured it was safer because I'm just not used to driving at night yet. Uh, do you really have to? I won't do it again, honest!"

His handsome face creased into a small smile. "Sorry, miss, you broke the law. I have to. Now, don't ever do this again. Stick to the back roads if you want to drive slow. Does your friend drive?"

When we both nodded yes, he told Donna to drive the rest of the way, then took off. Still shaken, I glanced down at the traffic ticket. "Twenty-five dollars!" I wailed. "My folks will kill me! Damn! Donna, I'm probably the only person in the whole state who ever got a ticket for *not* speeding!"

Mom and Dad listened intently as I nervously told them the story.

"He really gave you a ticket?" Dad exploded, enraged at the trooper, not at *me*, I realized, puzzled.

"Jim . . ." Mom put a restraining hand on Dad's shoulder.

"I broke the law, didn't I?"

"Yes," Dad agreed, "but—"

I cut him off. "Do you mean he shouldn't have given me a ticket because I'm deaf? He should have given me special treatment? He should have let me off?"

Neither of them spoke.

"Thanks, but no thanks, Dad! I want to be treated just like any other driver. I'm sorry about the ticket. I'll figure out a way to pay for it."

I waited for Dad to let me have it. Instead, they both looked at me for a moment, their eyebrows raised, then at each other. Finally, Dad said, "Not to worry, Peanut. You had to get your first ticket sometime. These things happen. After some more practice at night, you'll improve." Without another word he went back to his newspaper.

They weren't angry with me after all. Somehow I seemed to have come out ahead. Go figure it. Parents are weird.

12

■ "If I never see another hamburger again, it'll be too soon!" said Donna, walking into my room one evening. "*And* my feet are killing me."

"Who's killing you?" I asked, startled.

"No, no, I said my *feet* are killing me. They hurt from standing on the hard floor so many hours every day. *And* the smells! And the manager is a nasty jerk! And those stupid boys." She paused. "Except Jimmy, he's nice."

"Tell me!" I demanded.

"Nothing to tell really," Donna said, trying hard to be cool. "Jimmy kids around, and I think maybe he likes me, but can you think of any place less romantic than the kitchen of a hamburger joint?"

I tried, but I couldn't. "Well, not really," I admitted, grinning.

"Would you believe I've gained two pounds? Even after skipping lunch a couple of times. So I don't eat, and then comes supper, and I'm so starved that I eat everything in sight! It's a lousy job!"

"Still, it's a job, and it's not forever."

"Some days—" Donna stopped abruptly. "Sorry. Well, at least I know what I *don't* want to do ever again if I can help it. Want to go to the beach with me tomorrow, Jenny? I just want to lie around and soak up some sun."

"Sure, Donna, that'd be super!"

"Okay, I'll pick you up at ten."

"Fine, I'll pack us some lunch, salad and stuff—"

"Remember," Donna insisted, "nothing fattening. I'll bring some diet soda and fruit." She pulled herself out of the chair, eased her shoes back on, and left. Too soon, always too soon. But we'd have lots of time to gab tomorrow, I figured. Tomorrow, on the beach, would be great.

"Tomorrow" turned out to be lousy. We got there early, found a lovely spot away from the mob, swam, and kidded around in the water for a while. Then, while Donna soaked up the sun, I unpacked our lunch. We finished eating and got into position to talk. When Donna lay down, I had to bend way over to read her lips, so we sat with our legs crossed, Indian style.

In the middle of a sentence Donna suddenly flashed a big smile, sat up even straighter, and waved to someone behind me. I turned around and saw a group of kids coming toward us. A tall, skinny boy was leading them, waving and grinning.

"Who are they?" I asked.

"It's Jimmy! Jimmy and Hank and some others that I don't know. Remember, I told you about Jimmy, the guy I work with?"

I nodded. I remembered. Before either of us could say another word, three boys and two girls descended on us. Jimmy introduced everyone to Donna. The boys spread their blankets next to us, and everyone plopped down with towels, beach balls, and assorted stuff. I waited, watching the moving lips and grinning faces. Jimmy's face was turned at a bad angle, and I couldn't understand what he said.

Donna smiled at everyone and then held up her hand. "This is my friend Jenny. She's deaf, so talk slowly please." Then she pointed to each one and said their names for me, finger-spelling when necessary. Everybody looked surprised, but they all waved or said "Hi" and, after an uneasy pause, sprawled around. Jimmy sat next to Donna, opposite me.

"Uh—were you born deaf?" he asked.

"No, I lost my hearing."

"How?"

I told him about the accident.

"Oh." He turned to Donna, and I caught a few words. He wiggled a few fingers, so I guessed he was asking her about finger-spelling. She started to answer, then said, "Jenny, you explain."

I did by showing him a few letters. Then, forgetting, they both spoke too rapidly for me to understand. Donna threw her head back, and they both laughed.

"What's so funny?" I asked.

"Jimmy just made a crack about a guy at work. It's not important," Donna said. As soon as she finished, others clustered closer, and the conversation really got rolling. Lips moved quickly, heads rolled back, and shoulders shook, hands gestured, mouths opened wide, then moved rapidly again. Hank was pushed off the blanket for some unknown crime. My eyes took it all in. I caught a word or a phrase a couple of times, but that was all. I kept on trying. It was no use.

A couple of the guys pulled one girl up, and they raced off to swim. That left a girl named Lisa, Jimmy, Donna, and me.

"Lisa, do you go to Stevens High?" I asked.

"Yeah," she answered. "Do you? Haven't seen you around."

"I did. I'll go back soon, probably in the fall."

"What's the rush? I wouldn't go at all if I didn't have to!" she said, and laughed. Then, turning her back to me, she said something to Jimmy and Donna, and all three laughed harder.

After getting his breath back, Jimmy spoke very quickly, and Donna responded. I caught "you" . . . "Jenny" . . . on her lips but lost the rest.

I wanted to scream: *Why are you talking about me as if I'm not here, Donna? What's the matter with you? I* wanted to say, *Help me! We came together, remember?* I didn't. I couldn't get the words out.

Before I could get up the nerve to interrupt, to say something, the swimmers returned, dripping water and spraying sand. They toweled each other off and collapsed on the blanket.

The guy next to me turned on a radio. Soon hands clapped rhythmically and bodies rocked gently, so I knew they were listening to music. It must have been turned up very loud. The vibrations hurt my ears. Music had become, to me, either nonexistent or, as it was now, a harsh, vibrating noise that hurt my ears.

Nuts! I didn't need this! I wasn't going to bluff and pretend it was just great to be completely ignored a minute longer. I hated them, all of them, the thoughtless idiots!

I grabbed my towel and ran down to the water. I swam out, pulling against the waves, kicking hard, moving almost desperately, to burn away the rage and hurt.

I swam out until I began to tire, then slowly swam back to the shore. With a towel around my shoulders, I sat at the water's edge, letting the tail end of the waves lap at my toes.

Huddled there alone on the damp sand, I could breathe freely again. Alone, I felt safe, at ease.

Finally, I walked back to the group. I lay on my stomach, pretending to be half-sunning and half-napping. No one really noticed.

As I said, it was a lousy day. No one really meant to be unkind, I guess. They were just behaving as they always did, doing what was normal—normal when you can hear. But why couldn't they have tried a little? Just a little. Was that too much to ask? Maybe. And maybe all I should do at times like this was just play along. So I played the game because I had to. After all, it was the only game in town, or so I thought then.

The following day, I noticed a moving van in front of the small brick house down the road that had been unoccupied for months. A chubby red-haired girl stuffed into tight jeans was holding a little kid by the hand and carrying a large bulging sack into the house. Soon she was back for another one. She looked about my age, maybe a little older. Everyone looked busy, so I walked on, figuring I'd stop to say hello and welcome on my way back. When I passed by fifteen minutes later, the yard was empty. Disappointed, I headed home.

The next morning, when I reached the small brick

house, I saw the new girl picking up the mail. I speeded up and, when I reached her, a little short of breath, said, "Hi! I'm Jennifer Greene. I live up the road just a few blocks from here. Welcome to Millport."

We shook hands as she smiled and said, "I'm Anne, Anne Brent. Glad to meet you. I haven't had a chance to meet anyone, we've been so busy!"

She spoke so quickly that I hadn't caught anything but her name. "Hold it, Anne," I said. "I didn't catch what you said after your name. I'm deaf."

"Oh! I . . . I'm sorry!"

"Don't be. Just talk a little slower. It takes time to lip-read someone new."

"I said, 'Glad to meet you. We've been so busy,' " she repeated, more slowly this time, looking at me questioningly. "Did you understand me?"

"Most of it. Enough. Where are you from?"

"California, L.A. Were you born deaf?"

"No. I lost my hearing in an accident."

"How awful!" Anne said. "Is reading lips very hard? It must be!"

Too fast again. I asked her to repeat. She did. "Sometimes it is," I told her. "It depends on lots of things—the light, the number of people you're trying to keep up with, the general conversation, patience on the other person's part, until you get the hang of it."

"Whew! I could never do it!"

"Sure you could if you *had* to," I said.

"Maybe." She looked very doubtful.

"Look, would you like to come over to my house after lunch or later in the afternoon?" I asked.

"I can't. There's still so much to do."

"Tomorrow then?"

She shook her head, then said very slowly, "I'm sorry, I . . . don't think so. Mom made some plans. I'll stop by when I get a chance, all right?"

"Sure!"

"Mom's waiting for the mail," Anne said. "Bye, I'll see you around." With a wave she hurried off.

It wasn't until I reached the huge maple a few yards from our house that I realized she hadn't even asked where I lived.

Smokey was asleep in my lap; the phone was glued to my ear. Donna gabbed away about her job, about Jimmy, the jokes he pulled to relieve the monotony, about the other kids she worked with and the kooky people who sometimes came in. I giggled as I got the details, commenting and questioning, relaxed and happy. We talked on and on, and then somehow the phone turned to jelly! It slipped from my fingers, and I couldn't get hold of it. I kept trying to, but my hands trembled. I couldn't make them stop shaking.

I woke up abruptly, unable to see for a moment in the darkness. Oh, God! It was only a dream, so real but only a dream!

The pillow was real, and me in my bed. I wept. I hugged the pillow and wept because it was only a dream. Such a lovely dream, so simple, so *good*. It was as it had been once upon a time. As it had been then, not as it was now. And I couldn't change it to then, no matter how much I wanted to. Oh God, will I ever stop wishing I could hear?

13

■ It had been a hot, sticky Saturday. The early-morning drizzle stopped, it cleared briefly, and then the rain started again. Like a shy kitten, the sun had sneaked out and back again every so often.

It was still light when Mom and Dad left to meet friends for dinner and the theater. They had not gone willingly. They hated leaving me home alone. But I had protested that (1) they needed to get out more; (2) I needed time off from *them*; and (3) I was perfectly safe —the house wasn't going to burn down. It was time they trusted me, I'd said. They finally agreed. The real clincher was that I was dog-sitting Champ, our neighbors' shepherd, for the weekend and making some money doing it. Champ and I had been buddies for years. He's a well-trained guard dog. We all knew I couldn't be safer with a platoon of marines. Smokey, of course, scooted up and perched on top of the kitchen cabinets when Champ was around and rarely came down.

Champ and I fooled around out back, with him fetching sticks and balls and stuff. After I'd made supper for all of us, putting Smokey's dish on top of the refrigerator, I settled into a comfortable chair with Champ at my feet. He responded to every command I gave him immediately. Later, as I reached for a book, Champ sat bolt upright, ears raised and quivering, then darted off.

"Champ, come back!" I called. He didn't respond. What was with him? I wondered. Seconds later he ran to my side, looked up at me, and barked several times. Not only could I see his jaws move, but I also felt the vibrations of his bark.

"What? What do you want, boy? What's the matter?" I asked, puzzled. He dashed away again and was back moments later, barking at me insistently.

"Okay, okay, you're trying to tell me something, but *what?*" When he ran off again, I followed. Champ stopped at the front door, turned to me, and barked again. Our front door has glass panes on the sides, so I peeked out and suddenly understood. We had a visitor, and Champ had found a way to tell me! A dark-haired guy, in faded blue jeans and a T-shirt, stood there, pressing the bell.

"Good boy!" I said as I patted Champ's head. Now what? I wasn't supposed to open the door for strangers. He didn't look menacing, though. Champ was right beside me, and when I saw the words "Stop Noise Pollution! Use Sign Language!" on his T-shirt I threw the door open, grinning like an idiot.

"Stay!" I ordered Champ.

"You're Jenny, right?" His lips formed the words, his finger pointed to me. Then he spelled out my name. He extended his hand, which I shook. He patted Champ's head.

I understood the simple words. The signs told me who he had to be. The broad grin reassured me, helped me get the words stuck in my throat out. I spoke carefully. "Yes, I'm Jenny. You must be Joe Benton. Please come in. I'm so glad to meet you!" He moved his closed fist down twice and finger-spelled his name, and I sighed with relief. He *was* Joe Benton, the deaf guy Ellen had told me about. Mentally I apologized to my folks, who would have killed me for opening the door to a perfect stranger! There were times you had to take risks, I figured, some risks anyway.

We sat comfortably facing each other, with Champ at ease but watching carefully. Joe patted Champ's head. "Glad to meet you, too, Jenny," he said. "Nice dog."

"Thanks, he's not mine. I'm taking care of him for the folks next door. I'm sorry, I don't know how to sign. I've only learned a few signs. Can you lip-read me?"

"Sure. How about you? Can you understand me?"

"I think so, but could you talk just a little slower until I get used to your speech?"

"Okay, but you really *must* learn to sign," he said.

I must? I'd just met this guy, and already he was giving me orders! Well, maybe he didn't mean it that way. "Why?" I asked. "Why must I?"

"Because . . . for lots of reasons! Can you lip-read everybody?"

"No. Can you?"

"No way! And I've been doing it all my life!"

"Oh."

"And even a very good lip-reader makes mistakes sometimes," he continued. "But if you learn sign language, you can understand almost all deaf people, too. Sign is one more way of communicating. Sign, lip-read, finger-spell, talk, write, use everything!"

"You mean, use whatever helps you understand each other?"

"That's right."

"That makes sense. But isn't it hard to learn?'

"Not so hard if an expert shows you, teaches you."

"Are you an expert?" I asked, smiling.

"Sure," he said, grinning. "Both my parents are deaf. My father lost his hearing when he was four. My mother was born deaf. I learned to sign when I was very little. Then later I learned to lip-read. Now I use both together."

I realized it was harder for me to lip-read him when he signed at the same time. His moving hands distracted me from his lips and face. I didn't know where to look!

"Joe, could you talk to me without signing for a while, please?" I asked. "It's easier for me to understand you. I'm not as good a lip-reader as you are."

"Sure," he replied, dropping his hands into his lap. "I understand. Would you like me to teach you to sign? It really isn't hard."

I would have done anything to keep him talking, so I made a lightning decision and said, "I think so. I know a few signs. My folks and I learned them when Dad taught me to drive." I showed him the few signs I knew.

"Hey, that's good. Very good!" he exclaimed, his whole face lighting up. You'd think I just handed him a gold medal or a ticket to the World Series or something!

"I could try to learn," I said, encouraged.

"I'll teach you," Joe said. "We'll go slow. I'll be very patient, I promise."

"Tell you what," I said. "Let's make a deal. There's so much I want to learn about deaf people. How about if we sign half the time and the other half we just talk? It's easier for me right now and faster. Okay?"

"Okay, if it's more comfortable for you that way. You do have to keep up your lip-reading, too."

I wasn't really putting him on, I told myself. Learning to sign was probably a good idea, but mostly I wanted to see him again, get to know him better. With his warm, friendly smile and patient, careful speech, plus his easy-to-understand mouth, I wouldn't have traded him for the handsomest movie star!

He was staring at me now, frowning a little. I'd been too busy thinking, plotting. If he'd said something else, I'd missed it completely.

"Sorry, Joe, I missed what you said. Repeat it for me, please," I said.

"Okay. I can come over again some night next week after work if you want me to."

"Of course I want you to! Any day you can come over is fine. What kind of work do you do?" I asked.

"Gardening. Planting, cutting grass, and pruning mostly. I am working at the nature center for the summer. They are putting in more small flower gardens this year. I like working with plants," he added shyly.

Champ, who'd been still as a statue, rose to his feet and barked at me urgently. Then he ran to the door, raced back, and barked again. "Excuse me for a minute," I said, and let Champ out quickly.

Returning, I found that Smokey had appeared from out of nowhere and decided to investigate my guest. To my surprise, she rubbed up against Joe's leg, then rolled over onto her back, waving her paws in the air, looking up at him expectantly. He grinned, dropped down on his knees, and rubbed her belly gently. She wriggled in ecstasy, then flipped over so he could stroke and scratch her back. He stroked her gently, then turned his face to me. "Got a large piece of newspaper?" he asked.

"Paper?"

He nodded. I ran into the kitchen and brought him some paper. He tore a large sheet in half, crumpled it up, and rubbed it over the rug several times. Then he held it in front of Smokey and slid it across the room. She took off after it, moving as if she had just sprouted wings. When she caught up to the paper ball, she pounced on it, then shoved it away with her paw, then pounced on it again. This new game was obviously all kinds of fun. We both grinned at her delight.

"What did you do?" I blurted out before I realized that Joe's face was turned away from me. I moved into his line of vision, and he looked up. I repeated my question.

"Old trick," he told me. "When you rub the crumpled paper on the carpet, it picks up electricity and makes noise when you throw it."

Makes noise? How could he know? My amazement must have shown on my face. I was beginning to catch on. Joe watched faces as well as mouths and hands to get meaning. He watched me intently as I spoke and even more when I didn't speak.

He sees more than I do, I thought.

"My father taught me that trick," Joe said. "We've always had a cat around. Dad is a chemist for National Pharmaceuticals. He's worked for them for over twenty years. He's been head of the department now for the last ten years."

"Oh! He must be a brilliant man!"

"We think so," Joe said proudly. "I want to be a

94

scientist, too. It's a good field for deaf people. You have to be smart and work hard, but not hearing doesn't matter much."

"Really?"

"Sure. Did you know that a deaf man won the Nobel Prize in chemistry in 1975?"

"The Nobel? You're kidding!"

"No, I'm not, Jenny. Dr. John Cornforth, a British scientist, won the Nobel. He lost most of his hearing in his teens. Later he became totally deaf."

I sat there with my mouth hanging open. Joe smiled at my astonishment. "Of course, not all deaf people are so smart! We vary as much as hearing people do. For those born deaf, it's a thousand times harder to learn to speak and read and write well. There are many who don't do these things well."

"Why not?" I asked.

"Jenny, think," Joe said, pointing to his right temple with his index finger. "Who taught you to talk?"

"Nobody. Mom said I just did it one day when I was about a year old."

"But your parents and everyone else around you talked to you from the beginning, didn't they?"

"Sure. Everyone talks to babies. It sinks in, and one day babies start to talk back. It's instinctive, we imitate, we talk . . ."

"Babies who *hear* talk."

"Of course." Suddenly I saw what he was getting at. A child talked by imitating the words, the sounds he *heard*. For a deaf baby, there *were* no sounds, no words to imitate—only lips and faces moving silently. All the thousands of words, phrases, and sounds kids were bombarded with from birth, all these were missing! A deaf baby could only watch and try desperately to make some sense out of his or her world. How terribly difficult it must be to understand the simplest things! And to make one's own needs understood must be even harder!

Joe touched my hand lightly to regain my attention. "Jenny, my aunt is a teacher."

"Is she deaf?"

"Yes. She told me that a five-year-old hearing kid has a vocabulary of about five thousand words." He paused.

"And a deaf kid of that age has how many?" I asked.

"Two or three hundred."

Stunned, I could only look at Joe and wince.

"In spite of that," he continued slowly, "there are deaf people who are artists, teachers, counselors, lawyers, mathematicians. . . ."

"Really?"

"Sure. Also biologists, researchers, administrators, actors, programmers, psychologists, printers and photographers, professors, businessmen—and lots of other things, too!"

"Please repeat that, Joe. I'm not sure I understood all of it." He did. "There are deaf people who really do *all* those things?"

"Yes, and more!" he said proudly. Then he glanced at his watch and said, "Sorry, Jenny. I have to go. Okay if I come over next Thursday night around seven-thirty?"

"Sure. Thursday is fine. It was awfully nice of you to come and to offer to help. There's so much I want to know! Thank you!"

"You're welcome! Maybe you can come over to my

house sometime. So long, see you Thursday at seven-thirty."

Champ and I walked with Joe to his car. He got in, waved, and drove off.

I hugged Champ hard. "You are a beautiful, brilliant dog!" I told him. "You figured out how to let me know he was here!" Lucky thing he had, too. It seemed that deaf people often just dropped by, taking the chance on finding people at home. Without being able to call on the phone, what else could they do?

Champ rubbed his head against my leg as we stood there together, feeling good. A cooling breeze made the leaves of the old maple dance. The haze had lifted, and a million stars lit up the sky.

14

■ "Jenny, Mrs. Gardner called," Mom said. "The lip-reading group begins soon. First class is Wednesday, September eighth at 10:00 A.M."

"Hey, that's super! How often do we meet and for how long?" I asked.

"Once a week, every Wednesday, for fifteen weeks," she replied.

"But what about school? That means I can't go back for at least another four months!"

"Jen, you have to be able to lip-read in a group before you can go back to school. You know that."

"But I'm missing so much already," I protested. "Now I'll miss even more. Besides, I'll go batty!"

"You don't have to miss the schoolwork, honey," Mom said. "You'll have a special teacher coming four days every week for two hours each day."

"Really? A teacher just for me?"

"Yes, I got a call just this morning. These are special teachers for the homebound, for those who aren't able to go to school, for whatever reason. They've assigned Mrs. Hutchins to you. I know her. She's a wonderful person and a dedicated teacher. You'll be able to make up everything and do the rest of this year's work as well."

I sat at the kitchen table, thinking. I wasn't ready to

go back to school, I knew that. I would have to put in a lot of time in a group setup, lip-reading strangers, switching from one to another. That would be hard. Deep inside, I knew I couldn't go back. Still, I felt awfully disappointed. In fact, I felt rotten.

School . . . I used to complain endlessly about the rules, the boring teachers, the Mickey Mouse courses, the things they *didn't* teach that we wanted and needed to know. But I missed the *good* teachers, who did turn you on, the classes that *did* come alive, the contact with all sorts of people and the exciting exchange of ideas. I wanted to go back badly.

Mom's hand touched mine and brought me back. "Yes, Mom?"

"Jenny," Mom said, "I know you're disappointed, but try to look at it this way. A one-to-one setup is the best kind of learning experience. You'll be able to go so much faster and do so much more. You'll have *all* your teacher's attention. We've also arranged for you to use Stevens' library and resource rooms two afternoons a week. Oh, and this came for you this morning from Mr. Stein."

I reached for the letter in her hand, eagerly. I read the brief note quickly and let out a yelp of joy. "Hey, Mom! Mr. Stein says he wants me to come in the last period on Tuesdays so we can work together! He's giving a course in creative writing that I'd planned to take this year. He thinks I should add it to my program with Mrs. Hutchins, and he'll tutor me! Isn't that fantastic?"

Mom grinned and nodded happily. "Looks as if you're going to have your hands full this year, Jen. Be good for you! I've got to go now, honey. There are quite a few things I have to pick up at the store this afternoon."

"Go on then. I'll finish cleaning up," I said, checking my watch. "Joe will be here soon, and I want to review some notes and signs in my book."

"All right. Take care, love," she said, and hurried out.

Joe arrived five minutes later, carrying a large, thick manila folder. "For you," he said, smiling, "to answer some of your questions and help you to understand deaf people better."

"Thanks! Come and sit down," I said, plunking the folder down on the coffee table and impatiently pulling out several copies of magazines called *The Deaf American* and *The Volta Review* and two newspapers, *The Silent News* and *The Broadcaster*.

I'd never heard of or seen any of them! "I can hardly wait to read them," I told him. "Thanks!"

"You're welcome. Now look, this is how you sign 'Thank you,'" he said, smiling. He put his palm with the fingers closed to his lips and then pulled it away from his face. It was the same gesture as blowing a kiss except his lips didn't move to say the words until after his hand left his face.

I made the sign and was rewarded with a big grin. This time his hand moved to his mouth and then down into the upraised palm of his other hand as he said, "Good!"

Again I copied his sign, saying the new word. Then he formed V with both hands, put the tips of his fingers together, and repeated "Good," saying, "Very good!" I smiled and signed that, too.

100

"Now repeat, do them again," he commanded. I did. He insisted that I sign what he had taught me three more times and then applauded when I got it right. We went through a dozen more signs, Joe insisting that he include the sign for "why" since that seemed to be my favorite word! Then he signed a few short sentences without moving his lips to make sure I understood. It was harder understanding what he signed than doing it myself. But he was patient and repeated each sign until I caught on.

"It would be good if you could practice with other people, Jenny," he told me when we called the lesson to a halt.

"But I don't know anyone else who signs," I pointed out.

"That's true," he said, raising a finger signaling me to wait. He sat silently, deep in thought for a few minutes.

Joe brightened suddenly. "Sometimes I am stupid," he said, touching his fist to his forehead, annoyed with himself. "I almost forgot. Would you like to see a movie, a captioned film? They're showing a good one Saturday night."

"A what? Did you say a movie?"

"Yes. Did you ever see a foreign film with the words people are saying across the bottom in English?"

"You mean films with subtitles? I've seen a couple—"

"Yes, subtitles. That's it! These are regular American movies with subtitles. *We* call the words captions. Captioned films are made especially for deaf and hearing-impaired people."

"Oh, Joe!" I said. "I haven't seen a movie in so long!

I thought I'd never, ever see one again! I can't believe it!"

"We show movies every month at St. Mary's Episcopal Church," Joe continued, smiling.

St. Mary's Episcopal Church? "But—but I'm Jewish," I said. "Well, not very, but—" Joe threw his head back and laughed.

"Who cares? Jenny, deaf people of all ages, races, religions, and no religion at all come. Everyone is welcome. You'll meet lots of people, and you can practice signing with them, too. We serve refreshments and talk after the movie. It's fun. I'll pick you up at six-thirty, okay?"

"Sure, I'd love to go! It sounds terrific. Wonderful!"

Before Joe could say anything more, Smokey, who had been curled up next to me, leaped up, ears quivering, and ran from the room.

"She must hear something," I said.

A moment later Mom entered, apologizing for being so late. Joe rose as I introduced them.

"Pleased to meet you, Mrs. Greene. Let me help," he said, taking several packages from her arms.

Mom looked at him oddly, then quickly said, "Thanks so much. I'm very glad to meet you, too, Joe." She smiled and gestured for us to follow her into the kitchen.

As we unloaded, I told her about the movies. "It's okay if I go, isn't it? You and Dad can do without me, can't you?" I teased.

"We'll manage somehow," Mom replied, deadpan. "Of course, it's okay, hon. It's great!" She smiled, carefully faced Joe, then said, "Tell me more, please, Joe."

"It's a federal program for the deaf. They send you a catalog. You pick the movies you want and the dates you want to see them. My father does that. Then you send in the order for a year at a time. After the showing we mail them right back so others can see them. Any group of six or more people can send away for captioned films." Joe caught the puzzled look on Mom's face and turned to me, "Did your mother understand me, Jenny?"

She hadn't. I could tell, too.

"Please interpret for me, Jenny." He finger-spelled the word to be sure I understood. Quickly I did. Mom thanked Joe apologetically, and he turned to face me again. "Please tell her it's okay. It happens all the time. People need time to get used to my speech." He waited as I told her that much, and when my lips stopped moving and I faced him once more, he told me to say it had been nice meeting her but he had to go. His final words were for me. "See you Saturday at six-thirty, Jenny. Take care."

With a wave and a smile he left.

My mother plunked herself into a chair with none of her usual grace, the bewilderment on her face testifying to her feelings.

"Mom, didn't you understand *anything* Joe said?" I asked.

"A little, a few words, but not enough to grasp his meaning."

"Don't be upset, please. Mrs. Gardner told me once that most deaf speech is difficult at first, but sometimes you can make it out after you get used to it. Joe said the same thing."

"I'm not upset. It just startled me so. It's . . . it's strange."

"What's it like?"

"Honey, it's hard to describe! Sort of a monotone, and many sounds aren't clear enough to understand, although it was obvious he knew exactly what he was saying." She was quiet for a moment. "It must be tremendously difficult to speak if you've never heard. He's really remarkable, that boy!"

"Isn't he?"

"Very. His parents must be special people, too. I'd love to meet and talk with them." She frowned. "I suppose if I didn't understand them, they could write, don't you think?"

"Sure, and Joe's sister, Kathy, hears. Joe says she often acts as interpreter for him and his folks."

"Fine. Then I'll get in touch with them soon. Those captioned films sound marvelous!"

"Don't they? And I'll get to meet other deaf people, too."

People, a whole bunch of new people all at once! Joe's parents would be there, too. Exciting, but scary, too. Would they understand me? Some surely would. Would I understand them? Joe would help, I knew. But it wasn't like an ordinary movie where you went in and left right afterward. It was a kind of social thing, too. And me with a closet full of jeans! Comfortable, but worn and kind of ratty! Straight out of left field then, it hit me.

"Hey, Mom, what'll I wear? It's not a party, no big deal, I guess, but Joe's never seen me in anything but a shirt and jeans." (I hadn't seen him in anything else either, I realized, but that was somehow different.) I wouldn't feel right. We had a date, well, sort of. "Mom, help! For Pete's sake, what'll I wear?"

I must have sounded desperate because my mother burst out laughing!

15

■ Thick clusters of ivy climbed gracefully up St. Mary's ancient stone walls. Towering trees shaded it protectively. St. Mary's was a beautiful church, obviously built with great care a long time ago.

Joe parked in back of it. Only steps away were a pair of thick weathered oak doors. Joe pulled hard to open them for us. I followed him down a short flight of stairs that brought us to the center of a huge paneled room, more than fifty feet long. From the far wall a stocky man was rolling a full-sized movie screen down from the ceiling. Beyond that wall and to the right was a gleaming steel kitchen with an open pass-through counter.

Several people were arranging chairs in rows in front of the screen. Behind the last row, a steel table held the projector and reels of film. Joe took my hand and introduced me to his father, who was about to load the projector.

Mr. Benton, a tall, handsome man, greeted me with a warm smile, then quickly excused himself. Since his eyes and hands were busy skillfully threading the film through the machine, communication was impossible.

Small groups of people stood around, talking, signing rapidly, often laughing. Joe introduced me to his mother and to Barbara Adams, a pretty blond girl. We had time to exchange only a few words when someone flicked the light switch off and on several times. Everyone settled down quickly as the room was plunged into darkness.

The title *Little Big Man* flashed on the screen. I missed the actors' names as several of us shifted around a little so nobody's view would be blocked.

On the screen some Cheyenne braves attacked a small wagon train, taking two children captive. Minutes later, years had passed; the boy was now a young man. A wild thrill shot through me as I recognized him. "Hey! Wow! That's Dustin Hoffman!" I blurted out. "Oh!" Then, too late, feeling like an idiot, I clasped my hand over my mouth.

My eyes searched the intent figures around me. No one had moved. No head turned toward me or looked around, annoyed.

Whew! I relaxed, thrilled over and over again as the exciting story unfolded. All the dialogue was printed at the bottom of each frame just as Joe had described it. I could understand everything! All at once I was insanely happy. Even when my eyes filled up at the terribly sad parts, deep inside the gladness stayed with me.

And the thought that there would be other times like this and people to share them with felt wonderful. I could hardly wait to tell Donna all about it when we got together at her house the next night.

"Jenny, you didn't!" Donna exclaimed.

"I did, too. I went to a movie. Joe took me," I told her, pleased at her surprise and excitement.

"Which one? Tell me all about it. Everything!" she demanded, fully alert now, her arms clasped around her raised knees.

"It was fantastic! Like a good television play without commercials, only better. With only one projector, there were three intermissions while Mr. Benton changed the reels. During the breaks people stretched, moved around, and talked. A few had something to drink. Mr. Benton didn't rush, gave us time to chat for a few minutes."

"How many people were there?"

"About twenty or twenty-five, I guess. Most of them a lot older than Joe and me. And everyone was so friendly! After the movie was over, we helped ourselves to coffee, cake, or soda and sat around several large round tables, eating and talking."

"Could you understand?" Donna interrupted impatiently.

"Some. Not everyone. But I could lip-read several people, especially Barbara, a very friendly hard-of-hearing girl, a little older than we are. Joe introduced me to her right away, and either he or Barbara interpreted for a while when someone signed and I couldn't understand. Most people talked and signed. They all signed so fast!

"But the best thing was that they were all so friendly and accepting, so eager to teach me signs, to help me understand. When I found myself with a couple of people who were hard to follow, I'd simply sign and fingerspell, 'I don't sign very well yet, but I'm learning,' and that's all it took! It's an 'open sesame,' that sentence! Everyone grinned and signed, 'You're doing fine!'

"There was really only time to meet and talk with a couple of people, but I'll get to know others. I'm going to go to every film they show!"

"You should. It'll be fun, and you'll learn at the same time," Donna said. "Barbara sounds nice."

"She is. She's a little shy maybe, but I guess she felt comfortable with me because when I suggested getting together one day next week, she told me sure, she'd love to."

"That's wonderful."

"Isn't it? And, Donna . . "

"What?"

"Well, when Joe picked me up he . . . he looked kind of surprised and pleased. I was wearing my new skirt and ruffled blouse and sandals (instead of sneakers), and he told me I looked very, very nice. I . . . I felt pretty! I'm not, I know I'm not, but the look on his face, the way he said it, made me feel like I was!"

"This guy likes you, dope. He keeps coming over every week, takes you places, brings you stuff, and you really think all he cares about is teaching you sign language? He cares about *you*. Jenny, for a smart girl, you sure can be a dope!"

"Am I?" I shot back. "Well, maybe." I leaned back in the chair and thought about it. Could she be right? How was I supposed to know? I'd gone out a few times with one guy last year. Then he just sort of disappeared. There had been some parties, and often a bunch of us would hang around at the ice cream joint on Upton Road on weekends; but that was just buddy-buddy stuff really.

There was Tom. But though he'd been super to me, he was definitely not what you would call a boyfriend. There was Dan who'd asked me to the dance and then taken off for Tahiti for all I knew. Some track record.

Suddenly I became aware that Donna was waving her hand at me. "Hey, Jenny, look at me! What's with you?" she asked, frowning.

"Sorry," I told her, "just thinking. Maybe you're right about Joe. I hope so."

"Of course I am," she stated firmly. "Uh." She paused. "Does it matter so much?" she asked finally.

"Yeah. It does. I feel great when I'm with Joe. He . . . he understands."

"Figures," Donna said, smiling.

"Still seeing Jimmy, Donna? Does he still pull those crazy stunts?"

"Uh-huh. You should have seen the wild outfit he wore to history class last week. I thought Mr. Bronski would have a coronary!"

She told me more, and we talked on and on for hours. I wasn't really tired when we finally went to bed, but after five or six hours my eyes were beginning to hurt.

The next evening Joe had promised to come by for a signing session. I pulled on a clean pair of jeans and slipped a sweater over my head. Looking around, I was surprised not to see Smokey, who was usually rubbing my legs at this hour, asking to be fed.

I called Smokey. It was way past her suppertime. Usually she responded at once to my call. Not this time. I couldn't understand it. Leaving the door unlatched, figuring maybe she was out of reach of my voice, I walked up the long driveway, calling louder again and again.

"Smokey, Smokey! Suppertime!"

Drat that cat, where could she be? She'd never done

this before. Her inner clock never malfunctioned. By five o'clock, if I forgot, she'd appear from out of no-where to perch at my feet, face tilted up silently, de-manding her dinner.

I ran more swiftly, distinctly uneasy. I called her name again. Still no sign of her. As I reached our mail-box, I saw the headlights of Joe's Bug a couple of yards away pulled half off the road. He waved to me, signing to come. He'd flung off his jacket and was stooping down, reaching for something at the side of the road. I ran to him.

When I reached his side, I screamed, "Smokey! Oh, God! No!" She lay limp in his arms, eyes closed, blood trickling down from her mouth and covering half her body!

Joe motioned with his head to get into the car. I slid over to the right. He leaned over and gently placed her in my lap, then tipped my chin up. I thanked God for the overhead light in which I could see his mouth form-ing the words "She's alive! Hold on tight!"

With that, he slammed the door shut and hit the ac-celerator hard. He had left the engine turned on; we shot out onto the road. I cuddled the limp, bleeding body in my arms as we picked up speed. Horrified, but needing to know, I held my palm close to her nose and mouth. A faint touch of air grazed my fingers. She was breathing, but I couldn't tell where all the blood was coming from. Without knowing, there was no way to try to stop the bleeding. I held her as gently and firmly as I could, praying I wasn't hurting her more, cursing the monster who had hit her and left her.

There was no way of telling Joe *our* vet's name or

how to get there. Joe drove faster and faster. I closed my eyes and begged silently, *Smokey, Smokey, love, hang on, hang on. We're getting you help as fast as we can.* Within minutes we were on the main road headed downtown; the traffic was mostly going in the opposite direction. I glanced at the speedometer and saw that we were doing almost seventy miles an hour. Then I saw Joe press hard on the horn, warning the cars in front of us that we were coming on fast as he swung into the left lane. In another minute he slowed down and two blocks later he turned right. Another left brought us into the parking lot of a small brown-brick building, which I recognized immediately, only half seeing the large sign TWIN RIDGE ANIMAL HOSPITAL. Lights were on; it was still open!

Joe was out of the car in seconds, with me right behind him. He pushed the button and pounded on the door. The soft lights flared up brightly as the door opened. I breathed a sigh of relief at the sight of the portly white-jacketed figure motioning us to enter.

"Doctor, my cat is badly hurt; she was hit by a car. Please . . ." I couldn't say any more, nor could I understand what he was saying; but I realized that he recognized Joe as he waved for us to come in quickly.

"I'll do what I can. Wait here, please," he said, taking Smokey gently from my arms.

We sat on the couch in the waiting room with me still clutching Joe's blood-soaked jacket. I rolled it up into a ball and looked at Joe.

He took my hands in his and held them tight. I took a deep breath and forced my lips to form the words without trembling. "Oh, Joe, she's hurt so badly. I . . . I . . ."

"Look at me, Jenny," he commanded. "Dr. Winters is very good. I've known him for years. No one could do more. We've done all we can. Try to hang on. All we can do now is wait."

"I know."

My hands clenched into fists, unclenched, then curled up again tightly—so tightly that my nails cut into my palms. I found myself praying silently. I'm not sure God is around much these days, but in hospital waiting rooms, who else is there to turn to?

Please, please, God. I know she's only a cat, no, she isn't really only a cat, you see, she's such a very special cat. She never gets mad or impatient. She understands me better than people do now. She doesn't care if I can't hear anymore. She accepts me and loves me unquestioningly. Oh, God, please, please don't let her die....

The tears started to well up, but I blinked them back as I suddenly remembered. "Oh, Joe, our folks don't know where we are! Mom will come home and find me gone. She'll be worried. We have to call—but how?"

"Jenny," he said calmly, "the receptionist isn't here or the doctor wouldn't have come to the door himself. He was just about to leave. My folks won't worry. They know if I'm late there's a good reason."

"But mine will," I told him.

"When Dr. Winters and his assistant are finished, he'll call. All we can do is wait."

I knew he was right, but waiting can be so hard. I've always been a lousy waiter, wanting things to happen right away, if not sooner. It was one more thing I'd have to learn: to wait, patiently. I tried.

I tried not to think of how she'd looked, the limp feel

of her, the fur all matted with blood that kept coming out of her. I remembered her as a kitten, the day she'd jumped high into the air and caught her first fly, and my surprise when, after poking it questioningly, she ate it!

Joe got up and brought over a couple of magazines, handing me one silently. I signed "Thanks" and turned the pages halfheartedly. Pictures of beautiful healthy animals, mostly purebred dogs and cats in vivid color, stared out at me. Many had fancy titles and even fancier names: best of show, blue-ribbon winners—a very snooty crew. I tried to read an article, "What Every Pet Owner Needs to Know." When I finished it, I couldn't help looking at my watch again. They had been working behind that closed door for thirty minutes. I forced my eyes back to the printed page. It was no use. I saw the words, but they had no meaning. I couldn't read. I got up to see what else might be in the stack of papers and pamphlets on the table.

As I rose, the door opened, and Dr. Winters moved swiftly to me. Joe leaped to his feet, too. I looked into his face, and I knew, even before he took my hand in both of his and spoke. "I'm so sorry. She lost too much blood. Both legs and hips were smashed. We couldn't save her."

His face blurred as my eyes filled and overflowed. Instinctively I closed them, held my face in my hands and, half-choking, forced out a few words. "Thanks for trying. Would . . . would you please call my parents?" He nodded.

I don't know how long I cried, only that within seconds Joe's arms were around me and my head pressed into his shoulder. I reached up and put my arms around him and held on tight.

Then a large soft handkerchief was thrust into my hand as a gentle hand patted my shoulder.

I let go of Joe finally, sniffled, and blew hard several times. I wiped the last tears away, and looked up at Joe.

"Dr. Winters has called our folks, Jenny. Are you all right?" he asked.

"I . . . I think so."

"Then come," he said, taking my hand. "I'll take you home."

I thanked Dr. Winters again and returned his sopping handkerchief.

For once the silent ride home didn't matter. I sat close to Joe, and he squeezed my hand now and then.

Mom and Dad were waiting. The door opened wide as Joe pulled up. I signed "Thank you," waved good-bye, and threw myself into the closest open arms, my mother's, and cried some more.

My father's hand tapped mine very gently, then touched my cheek. I looked up to see him say, "It's awful, Peanut, but there are so many kittens who need a home. Maybe tomorrow you and Mom can go to the animal shelter . . ."

"You don't understand at all! I don't want another cat! There'll never be another Smokey. Never! Leave me alone!" I screamed as I ran wildly to the safety of my room and slammed the door hard.

16

■ Almost before I knew it, most of the trees were bare
and the snows were upon us. Soon there were days at a
time when the world turned into a sparkling fairyland. It
didn't last long; the plows cleared the roads within a day
or two at most. I was grateful for the clearing because
walking was possible once more, and places we had to get
to were accessible again. Yet I always missed the magic
white blanket that wiped away the eyesores of our city
for a little while.

A few times Joe and I hauled out sleds and coasted
down the icy steep slope on Willow Road. On the really
bad days we drove as little as possible or not at all.

Joe had gotten chains for his Bug and very rarely
missed our regular sessions. It took one of the worst
snowstorms in years to keep him away. We usually got
together on weekends, too.

One Saturday I tried to sign "Help," using both
hands. Joe shook his head. "No, not right. The other
way." Quickly he moved to the sofa beside me. "Curved
right hand under curved left hand; then move hands
up." He demonstrated, then placed my hands in the
proper positions and gently pushed them up. When he
dropped my hands, I made the sign correctly. It was the
mirror image that had confused me, which hand to use
which way.

"Good. Very good. We've time for a few more."

"Joe, how do you sign 'hearing'?" He pointed to his ear with his index finger, then moved it away. A real easy one—hurray!

"And the sign for 'deaf'?"

"There's a new sign for 'deaf,' " he said as he covered his ear with the palm of one hand and then brought both hands down together, thumbs touching. I copied the second motion, which meant closed or shut.

"What did you mean by 'new' sign, Joe?" I asked.

"The old sign was hand over ears, finger on closed mouth. Remember, not all deaf people are mute, only some. Most of us can speak, even if hearing people don't always understand what we say. So the new sign is for what we *are*—people with ears closed."

"I see. But aren't there some deaf people who have never learned to speak?" I asked.

"Of course. Also some who don't sign or only a little."

"Like me?"

"There are some who were taught only to speak and read lips, and many of the older people who lost all or a lot of their hearing often don't try to learn."

"Sometimes it's hard," I told him. "*I know . . . I know* I have to keep practicing." He nodded his head in agreement, and I caught sight of a tiny plastic button in his ear that I hadn't noticed before since his hair curls over his ears. "Oh, you wear a hearing aid. How come?"

"I can hear some sounds with it."

"Sounds? What kinds of sounds?"

"A telephone ringing if I'm very close to it, a church bell sometimes, or just a noise. I can tell when you are speaking. I hear and feel the vibrations of your voice if I

am close enough to you." As I looked at him wonder-
ingly, he continued, "Like me, many deaf people have a
tiny little bit of hearing."

"The human voice? A yell or a shout?"

"No," he said firmly. "I can't hear words or voices.
Some can a little bit." He paused. "Jenny, what is hearing . . . what is it like to hear?"

A chill ran through my body, and for a moment all I
could do was gasp at the immensity of his question.
Where could I find words to describe voices, whispers,
shouts, laughter, or music? I stalled, buying time. "Let
me think a minute, Joe, please."

"Sure."

He wanted so badly to know. He deserved some kind
of honest answer.

"Well, hearing makes understanding easy," I said finally. "You don't have to do anything or make any effort
at all, not even the tiny effort you make when you lift
your eyelids to see—sounds just come to you . . ."

I paused, then struggled on. "It's awfully hard . . . it's
almost impossible to explain. Could you explain color to
a blind person, someone who has never seen? What is
'red' like? You can say it's warm and bright and pretty,
but that doesn't help much, does it?"

"No, not much," he agreed. "Is . . . is *sound* pretty?"

"Sometimes. Sometimes it's beautiful. Sometimes it's
ugly, terrible, and it . . . it hurts."

"I know; some noises, some sounds hurt my ears."

"Mine, too. Even now . . ." The rest I couldn't say to
him—that I'd gladly take back all the ugly sounds if I
could have the others, too, if I could understand everything easily once more. He peered at me closely, sensing

that I'd left something unsaid. One large firm hand closed over mine. With the other he tipped my chin up toward his face.

"What is it, Jenny? What are you thinking?"

I couldn't answer. How could I even begin to explain how my world had changed, how sound had added a dimension far beyond its physical reality? I hadn't realized that until I lost it. Do we never comprehend how much we have until it is gone? I didn't.

Joe waited for the words that didn't come. When he could wait no longer, he touched my hand lightly and said, "Sound is good. You valued your hearing, right?"

Valued? Oh, God, it was so much more than that! Still, there was no way to tell the wonder of it. I didn't try. He guessed. He sensed it, I knew that. "Yes," I said simply.

"I understand, I think," Joe said slowly. "There was a boy, a friend at my school for the deaf, a smart boy. One day he showed me a story in the newspaper about an operation for the deaf to give hearing. He wanted to know if it was true, could they do that? It's called a . . . a cochlear implant—supposed to bring sound directly to the brain. He was so excited! When I told him that I didn't think it was true because my father had explained to me that it was very experimental—it hadn't worked as yet, may never work—he . . . he got very, very angry. Then he . . . Jenny, he cried. He wanted to hear so much!"

A shudder swept through me. How could you miss something you'd never known?

"And you, Joe? Did you ever feel that way?"

He didn't answer. He sat back, cupped one hand to

his chin, and gave my question the deep serious consideration he always gave the rough ones. It was his way. Me, I always spoke too quickly, the thought and the words bursting through simultaneously. Joe didn't do that. When he was sure, he answered promptly, with certainty. Otherwise, he took his time.

"Maybe," he said finally, reluctantly. "It would be good to hear, I guess. But even more important, I want to communicate, to understand. There are so many important things to learn." He paused again. "I wish people could understand me better, try harder to," he went on. "I used to hate to write when people didn't understand. But now I don't mind much. It's better to write and ask them to write than not to find out what I need to know. I try . . . I keep on trying . . ."

"So do I. We have to. But many of them don't. Sometimes," I said, "hearing people are a royal pain in the neck!"

Joe threw back his head and laughed. "You're right, Jenny. Hearing people often are."

We share anger, too, then, I thought. *Anger at all those who can't or won't try to understand us, don't we? Joe,* I thought, *you teach me so much more than you know. It must have been hard to say that straight out, that you, too, never having heard, want to and, even more, want to understand, just like everybody else.*

Joe waved his hand before my face. My lips hadn't moved for just a little too long. He knew I'd slipped away into private thoughts again, as I sometimes did without meaning to. "Sorry, Joe," I said.

"That's okay. What were you thinking?"

"That it helps to know other people feel the frustrations and the anger, too. Thanks for telling me, for being honest about it."

"It's hard not to be honest with you, Jenny. You ask some tough questions, but you make me think."

Touched, I reached out and put my hand over his. "I'm so glad. You make me think, too, Joe, and see things I never saw before."

Joe covered my hand with his other hand and beamed. And so we sat for a few moments in silence until suddenly I remembered and blurted out, "Oh, I'm stopping you from signing!"

"We don't have to sign *all* the time, do we, Jenny?" he said.

Before I could answer, Joe drew me into his arms and kissed me gently and deeply. When we pulled apart, he seemed to want to say something but couldn't. Neither could I. For once neither words nor signs were necessary.

17

■ As my signing improved, I taught some key signs to Mom, Dad, and Donna. It helped me understand them better, especially Dad. The times Joe and I spent together changed. We began to reverse roles. Sometimes he was the teacher, and sometimes I was.

One afternoon, chores finished, I sat trying to read, trying to push thoughts of Smokey away. I felt the vibration of a thump. I looked toward the door.

"Jenny, you have a visitor. Joe's here," Mom said.

"Joe?" I dropped my book on the table. *How come?* I thought. *He usually works after school on Fridays.* "Oh! His jacket! Is it dry yet? I was going to drop it off at his house earlier if you didn't need the car, but I forgot."

"It's dry," she said with a little smile.

Joe was waiting for me in the living room. "Hi!" I said, handing him the jacket. "I'm sorry, I meant to bring it over earlier—"

"That's okay," he said. "Come on, Jenny, we're going for a ride."

"Huh? Where? Don't you have to work today?" I asked.

"No, I switched days. There's something I want to show you. It won't take long. C'mon!"

Puzzled, I turned to Mom. "Okay if I go out for a while, Mom?" I asked.

Mom gave me her "What's going on?" face. She started to ask something, then changed her mind. "Sure," she said.

As he helped me with my coat, I turned to him. "Joe, thanks. Thanks for last week."

"Forget it," he said, smiling gently. "Let's go!"

It was a crisp, cold, bright day. When we reached the main road, Joe headed north. Soon we were past the parkway. Fewer houses dotted the countryside. The lawns and stretches of trees were still pristine white; only the evergreens lent dashes of color to the sparkling landscape.

I asked Joe where we were going when we stopped for a light. He smiled but refused to tell me.

About twenty minutes later we turned into a long, curving driveway. I hadn't even seen the small frame house from the road. As we pulled up to the door, he said, "The Coopers are friends; Kathy and Fern go to school together."

A tall black girl with huge dark eyes and a lovely smile greeted us and took our coats. She gestured us to follow her down a long hall. Just what was going on here? I wondered. What was Joe up to? A few minutes later I found out.

The kitchen was big, old, and breathtaking, its oak beams jutting out at least a foot from the ceiling. Brick lined the far wall; a white counter extended below the large window on our right. Joe joined Fern kneeling down beside a large cardboard carton beneath the counter. They moved aside to let me see into it.

Huddled in the corner on a piece of old blue blanket was a tiny coal-black ball of fur. Joe reached into the box, scooped the kitten up, and placed it in my hands. Its head lifted, and blue eyes opened wide. It shivered, then stretched out a paw and gripped my sweater with tiny claws. As its head lifted, I saw a little triangular splash of white on its throat. Small patches of white dressed its paws in miniature mittens. It was adorable!

Fern's hand tapped my shoulder. "He's ten weeks old," she said.

"He can't be! He's so incredibly little!" I protested. "All of him fits right into my cupped hands."

"Runt of the litter," Joe told me. "Last one. Nobody wants him. His mother won't feed him anymore."

"Oh."

"He'll never be a normal-size cat," said Fern. "Too bad we can't keep him, but we have two already. We put an ad in the newspaper, but no one called. He'll have to be put down."

"Kill him? Oh, no! You wouldn't!"

As I hugged him close and rubbed his silky fur, he flipped his tiny pink tongue out and licked my cheek.

"Too bad," Joe said with a perfectly straight face. "He's paper-trained and beginning to eat cat food. Strong and healthy, too. It's a shame!"

"You'd really put him down?" I asked, not believing her for a minute.

"Have to. Strays lead short lives of terror and starvation. We couldn't do that to him."

"I know." I hugged him closer, stroking his tiny head. His fur was unbelievably soft. Poor tiny, unwanted orphan. He held on tight.

"What's his name?" I asked Fern.

"Doesn't have one."

"Then I'll call him Oliver, after Oliver Twist. He was an orphan, too."

"Oliver Twist?" Joe said questioningly.

"Yes. From Dickens's story. Oliver was a little English boy who ran away from an orphanage. Beautiful book. They made a play out of it and a movie, too, I think. I wonder if it's been captioned?" I said.

"We'll check. If it is, we'll order it," Joe said.

"Oliver! That's a perfect name for him!" Fern said gleefully. "You're taking him then, Jenny?"

"Sure." I turned to Joe, "You *knew* I would! He's irresistible, and he needs me. Can I take him right now?" I asked Fern, not wanting to let him go.

"Sure," she answered, picking up his blanket and wrapping it tightly around him.

"Thanks. Thanks so much. He's a darling. You're very kind. I'll take good care of him, I promise."

"I know you will, Jenny," Fern said as we left. "Good luck!"

We got into the car. I signed my thanks to Joe, but that really wasn't good enough! I felt so good that I just had to hug him. Then I planted a big kiss on his cheek. He put his arms around me, held me close, and kissed me hard. Suddenly, a needle-sharp claw raked my chin!

Oliver's tiny mouth was twisted in a wail. We'd forgotten him! "Ouch!" I yelped as we drew apart, laughing. "Sorry, kitten, we didn't mean to crush you, honest!" I told him. I stroked him gently all the way home.

Once we'd settled Oliver, Joe and I relaxed in the living room. *Here goes*, I thought, *now's a good time to ask. I have to know!*

"Joe, about school, what's it like?"

"Okay."

Just okay? He'd never minded my questions before. "Just okay?" I probed.

"Well . . . being on the team is great. It wasn't easy to get on it."

Joe enjoyed sports a lot, I knew, especially baseball, which, thank goodness, I understood and liked. I had watched him play.

"Why was it hard to make the team?" I asked. "You're a good athlete."

He grinned at me then and said, "Well, this is how it was, Jenny. I went out to the field for tryouts last spring with all the other guys. We waited and waited as the coach, Mr. Robbins, put each guy through a warm-up and made him show what he could do. It took hours!

"Finally, when it was my turn, he looked down at the sheet with our names on it, frowned, then looked at me and said, 'You're Benton, right? Uh—you're deaf, aren't you?'

"I looked him straight in the eye and said, 'Yes. So what?'

" 'Uh, I don't know. . . . I don't think we can use you, Benton,' he said, his face flushed.

" 'Why not? Do *ears* play ball?' I was mad as hell! Before he could stop me, I grabbed a bat from the rack and, stepping up to the plate, stared him down, saying, 'Let me try!' The other guys told me later what he said and how he just stood there a minute muttering, then called out to the team's leading pitcher, 'OK, pitch to him, Lenny!'

"While Lenny warmed up a little, I dug in at the plate, concentrating on getting control. I'd done well at my other school, and Dad and I had been practicing whenever we could.

"The first pitch was high and wide, way outside. I let it go by. The second pitch was way too low. 'Get it inside, Lenny!' Coach Robbins yelled. By that time everybody was clustered around, even the guys who were about to go home. Lenny wound up real slow, his left arm going all the way back, and I knew this was it. I never took my eye off that ball! I swung hard. Crack! I could feel the vibration of the impact as my bat connected."

Joe paused and smiled broadly, remembering.

"Go on!" I begged.

"Well," he continued, "it was a long fly to deep left field, way over the fielder's head. Would have been a home run in any regular ball park!"

I clapped my hands and yelled, "Yay! And then what happened?"

"The next couple of pitches I hit pretty good, too. All the guys were cheering, and that settled it. Coach Robbins really didn't have any way out. I made the team. Actually, he was nice about it after he got over the shock. He was just as excited as everybody else."

"That's wonderful, Joe!"

"Yeah. Being on the team is great. I've even taught a couple of the guys some signs."

"And the rest of school, the classwork, the teachers, how about that?" I asked.

"Okay." Again just one word.

"C'mon, level with me," I pleaded. "It's important. Mom says at Stevens the hard-of-hearing and deaf kids are in regular classes of twenty-five to thirty most of the time. Are there any interpreters or teachers who sign?"

"No."

"Any note takers?"

"No."

"Any special small classes or tutors?"

"Three times a week, two or three of us work with a speech teacher. Sometimes she'll tutor whoever she thinks needs it. We also meet with the school psychologist once a week. That's it."

"Can you understand the teachers?"

"Some of them, sometimes. I sit right up front. I guess the others do, too."

"Do you mean you're not together in any classes? You're the only one in your classes who is deaf?"

"Most of the time. Look, Jenny, there aren't that many of us. With kids of different ages, taking different courses, that's how it works out. In some subjects like art and physical education, it's not bad." He stopped again.

"But in the academic subjects, in history, English, math, or science—come on, Joe, how much of what's going on can you understand?"

"Okay, Jenny, you want it straight?"

"You know I do!"

"Not much! It's hell!" he answered furiously, making an *h* with his hand and rapidly slashing it across his chest. The sign expressed how strongly he felt as intensely as any voice would.

"I try to catch what the teachers say," he went on. "I get a little with some of them. With others, nothing! In a class discussion, forget it! I can't understand what I can't see!

"In math, it's not too bad because I can lip-read Mr. James pretty well. He lectures mostly, and we use the blackboard a lot and our text. But you can ask for a repeat just so often. Nobody likes interruptions. I caught on to that fast. I go home and read and reread and study hard. My folks or my sister, Kathy, help. But it's frustrating as hell! And boring! A hell of a lot of the time I'm just bored to death!"

"But if you miss so much, if you can't share ideas and opinions and viewpoints with your teachers and class-mates . . . if all you do is read and study on your own . . . Joe, that's *crazy*—that's not school; that's *prison!* Even worse, it's a prison where you can't even communicate with others!"

"That's the way it is, Jenny. You asked! You get used to it when you have to. . . ."

"But why? Why do you have to? Why didn't you go to the school for the deaf, Joe?"

Joe sighed deeply. "Jenny, I've gone to schools for the deaf since I was five years old, for almost ten years. I want to live at home with my family! Besides that, a lot of the work wasn't hard enough for me."

I just stared at him, speechless. After a moment Joe looked at me intently and said, "I'm going to college, Jenny. I'm not sure where yet. Maybe to Gallaudet, like my father did."

"I've never heard of Gallaudet. Tell me about it, Joe."

"Jenny, Gallaudet is the only liberal arts college es-pecially for the deaf in the world. It's in Washington, D.C. and named for Thomas Hopkins Gallaudet who started the first school for the deaf in the United States, right here in Connecticut over a hundred and fifty years ago. Until then nobody even tried to teach deaf people at all in this country!

"Anyway," he continued, "I intend to go to college. We figured a public school would prepare me better."

"How come?" I asked.

"Because even though schools for the deaf have much smaller classes, there are still usually too many students in a class for a really good discussion."

"Joe, how many students using total communication, sign and speech, can communicate comfortably?"

He paused, took a deep breath, looked sharply at me, then said, "For a really good discussion, a real exchange of ideas, without an interpreter, five at most. The fewer, the better! What school has classes that small?"

"All our schools do!" I told him, outraged. "Mom told me. There are special classes for those who don't read well, for emotionally disturbed kids, and for slower kids. They have special small classes for lots of kids . . . hearing kids."

Slowly Joe said, "I didn't know about those other classes."

"It's not right," I went on. "It's not fair to have lots of small classes and special services only for hearing kids! What about deaf kids? They need small classes and special services too But if we don't complain, if we all bluff—"

Joe's puzzled face stopped me.

"Bluff?" he asked. "I don't know that word, Jenny. What does it mean?"

"To fake it, to *pretend* to understand, to make-believe," I told him.

"Oh, go on."

"That's not right either! We'll never be given the things we need to get a good education. Why don't you tell them you don't understand, Joe?"

Joe's mouth tightened. For a long time he just sat there tensely. Then, finally, his body relaxed, and he spoke. "You're a smart girl, Jenny, but sometimes you *don't* think. When *you* speak, everyone understands you easily. When *I* speak, my family and people who know me well understand. Others just stare at me as if I've just come from—from some other planet!

"When I was little, kids teased me and made fun of me. Once I got so mad that I beat up a boy who did that! So now I speak only when I have to with most hearing people and use gestures at the same time. Or if it's important, I write; I act it out and *show* them. I *do* ask for explanations, I *do* interrupt sometimes, I *told* you! You just can't keep doing that!"

I was so ashamed. I had forgotten! I felt so stupid!

"I'm sorry, Joe," I said. "Understanding you is easy for me. I forgot. I didn't realize—"

"Now you do," he said. Then thoughtfully, "But maybe you're not *all* wrong. We *should* let them know that we're not getting what we need. If others have small classes, we should, too. Maybe we need to fight for that and for some teachers who sign, too.

"You know," he continued, "it's bothered me for a long time, but we get so used to going along, doing it their way, the way it's always been done. After all, teachers and school officials should *know*. Or *do* they?"

At that he stopped abruptly as if surprised by his own question. His face revealed his self-searching. He wasn't asking me this one, I realized. I waited.

Then he spoke urgently and signed, but not in the slower, controlled movements he usually used to make it easier for me. His large, graceful hands signed swiftly, eloquently, pure poetry in motion.

"Jenny, the fact is that very few hearing people *do* know, and many don't even *want* to know. When kids can't take it, they drop out or switch to private schools or to schools for the deaf, and things just go on as usual. It *is* lousy, but, Jenny, what am I supposed to do, tackle the whole crazy system all by myself? I'm not Superman!"

"But what about the other kids?" I asked. "If we could all get together maybe—"

"What other kids?" Joe snapped. "There was *one* guy I knew last year; he graduated. There was another guy I wanted to meet but never had the chance to. He left school. I know a couple of other deaf and hard-of-hearing people in school. One I don't get along with; another is much younger. We see each other once in a while. That's it.

"Making friends is hard, Jenny. There are just too few of us, too far apart. Sometimes we get lucky. Somebody hears about a guy or girl from a friend or teacher or whoever and tells my folks or Kathy, and I can take it from there. As soon as I heard about you, I wanted to meet you. I came over as soon as I could, and I'm awfully glad I did!"

His warm smile lit up the world.

"Oh, Joe! So am I!" I told him. "So am I!"

For a moment we just looked at each other. Then he cupped my face in his hands and kissed me. Softly and sweetly at first, then long and hard.

We caught our breaths at last, but neither of us spoke. Somehow we didn't need to. Closing our eyes again, we moved together once more. I stopped thinking altogether.

After he'd gone, it took me a while to breathe normally again and even longer for my pulse to stop racing. Part of me was excited and feeling great; another part of me was scared to death by what Joe had said about school.

Joe had adapted to the insensitivity and injustices of the system over a lifetime. He knew no other world. But *I* did. He knew he was missing things; I knew just what and how much. And people. The way it was set up you could spend the whole day surrounded by people and only a fraction of it, if that, with any real human contact!

School was going to be rough. I didn't know if I could hack it. School. Oh, God, I'd forgotten! My assignment for my writing course was due the next day! I hadn't done more than think about it briefly. I was to write a poem, preferably about some personal experience or discovery. I'd been so caught up in my feelings and thoughts about Joe. I kept remembering his thoughtfulness, his face, the urgency of his words, his large, graceful hands. I had understood it. *All* of it. Even as what he'd said frightened me, I was aware of the thrill I felt *understanding*. Although I still couldn't manage with half his speed and grace, I knew I was getting better at it. It would come, the skill of using both sign and words together. Involuntarily my hands made the signs as I spoke. Again and again I signed as the phrases and words erupted from my mind.

I jumped up and grabbed a pen and pad to write them down. An hour and many pages later I had what I wanted. *This is for you, Joe,* I thought. I typed it up carefully, elated.

Tomorrow, I decided, *I'll not only give Mr. Stein the poem, but I'll sign and say it for him* because it was a new form, a Sign-Poem, meant to be spoken and signed. Music for *us* as well as everyone else.

18

■ "Hi! Just walk down the hall, Jenny," Joe instructed, standing outside the Bentons' open door. As I did, a light flashed on and off on the desk in the living room. Joe pressed the outside buzzer. Ahead of me another light blinked. It was coming from the kitchen. I caught a brief glimpse of still another flashing in the room at the end of the hall. It flashed three times, then stopped.

"Hey, that's terrific!" I said. "Is there a flasher in every room in the house?"

"Yes," said Kathy, who was home for the holidays. "My parents and Joe can tell that someone is at the door no matter where they are. We've another code, a continuous flash to signal when the phone is ringing, too. Come look. You've never seen a TTY, a teletypewriter, before, have you, Jenny?"

"No. Only pictures of it. How does it work?"

"The typed words are transmitted over regular telephone lines electronically and appear on either a paper tape or the screen of your machine. You simply read it and then type back your reply or question to the person you're talking to," Kathy said. "Here, I'll demonstrate it for you. Watch!"

She lifted the receiver off the telephone and placed it on top of the miniature typewriter, then dialed. A tiny red button flashed, and Kathy explained that it showed that the phone at the other end was ringing. After a few flashes it held a bright, steady light and words appeared in a line just above the keys. "JANE HERE GA," it said.

Kathy typed back quickly: "HI JANE. KATHY BENTON HERE. GLAD I FOUND YOU HOME. I'M SHOWING A FRIEND HOW OUR TTY WORKS. HOW ARE YOU? GA."

"FINE KATHY. PLEASE ASK IF YOUR DAD WILL BE AT THE MEETING NEXT THURSDAY NIGHT. GA.

"SURE. I'LL ASK HIM. HOLD ON A MINUTE."

Kathy got up and went to the study to check with Mr. Benton. Turning to Joe, I asked, "What does 'GA' mean?"

"Go ahead," he answered. " 'SK' at the end of a message means 'signing off.' TTY calls take much longer, so we use these short terms for many words."

"That makes sense."

"DAD SAYS HE'LL TRY TO BE THERE. GA," Kathy typed upon her return.

"GOOD. GLAD HE CAN MAKE IT. TELL HIM WE'LL SEE HIM THERE. TAKE CARE KATHY. SK."

"YOU TOO. SEE YOU. SKSK."

Joe touched my hand lightly, grinning broadly. "Isn't it great, Jenny?" he asked.

"Fantastic!" I assured him.

"The coupler, which hooks up the electronic typewriter to any phone, which makes the TTY possible, was invented by two deaf men years ago," he said. "Now there are thousands in use all over the country and more being installed every day."

Only the glorious odors coming from the dining room persuaded me to move from the TTY and visions of actually being able to use the telephone again!

We had barely finished dinner when Kathy jumped up

and answered the phone. When she was home, she answered when it rang. If there was only a deep silence or clicking when she picked up, she knew it was a TTY call and placed the handset on it. This time she listened to whoever was speaking, then quickly signed for her father to come. As she listened, she signed to him. I caught a few words: "Police" and "Can you come?"

Bill Benton winced. Alarm and dismay showed plainly on his face. He fired a question back at Kathy, who nodded in agreement and spoke again into the phone quickly.

What on earth was going on? I wondered. Joe's and his mother's faces echoed mine. Kathy quickly filled us in. "That was the Port Chester police. A couple of their men picked up a kid walking alone along the Merritt Parkway. They can't communicate with her. She won't talk or write. They think she may be deaf or retarded. They need an expert signer and asked if we could please help."

"Ten to one, she's deaf," Mr. Benton said. "Maybe hurt, too. They said she seemed dazed. Kathy and I are going now!"

"I'll come, too," Joe said.

His father nodded in agreement as Mrs. Benton signed: "Go quickly. That child needs help!"

"Please can I come, too?" I asked urgently.

Bill Benton hesitated, looked at me questioningly for a few seconds, then said, "All right. Come on!"

Within minutes we were on our way. The roads weren't too bad, and the traffic was very light. It was a wet, cold night. A *rotten* night to be out all alone. We drove past snow-laden trees, small houses and apartment buildings. Up ahead we could see one low-slung, brightly lit building at the center of a cluster of similar ones. As we got nearer, bright blue and white signs directed us to the police station.

As soon as Kathy told the sergeant at the desk in the lobby who we were, he directed us to a room down the hall. It was a small, bare room with a desk in each corner. At the nearest desk were two cops, one seated behind the desk, another perched on it's corner. In the chair at the side of the desk a small, skinny figure in jeans huddled, legs curled up to her chest, arms wrapped tightly around them, straggly blond head down, face hidden. Slowly she rocked back and forth.

Both men looked up quickly as we entered. The stocky gray-haired trooper perched on the desk leaped up, held out his hand, and greeted us, exchanging quick words with Kathy.

I couldn't take my eyes off the frail, trembling figure in the chair. Flinging his coat off, Mr. Benton touched her hand gently. Startled, she looked up quickly. God! She couldn't be more than ten years old. Ten years old and terrified!

Mr. Benton pulled the nearest chair over and sat, bringing him into eye-to-eye contact as we all positioned ourselves around the two of them. "Hello! Don't be afraid," his hands flashed. "Are you deaf?"

Her pale face lit up, and she released her knees to move her right-fisted hand down twice, quickly signing "Yes!"

"It's all right," Mr. Benton's hands told her. "We're deaf, too. I'm Bill Benton." Pointing to each of us, he told her who we were and finger-spelled our names. As they signed, Kathy watched closely and interpreted everything to the two fascinated policemen. I stood opposite her and watched her.

"What's your name?" Mr. Benton asked.

"Mary. Mary Smith," she spelled quickly, her grimy, tearstained face lifted to his trustingly.

"We're here to help you, Mary," Mr. Benton's hands said. "Where are you from? Where do you live?"

"Stratford," she told him reluctantly.

"Pretty town," he commented.

Mary frowned. She didn't seem to think so.

"How old are you?"

"Twelve."

Quick glances of surprise were exchanged. Twelve? It didn't seem possible.

"Tell me, Mary, what were you doing on the parkway?"

Mary looked away, lowered her hands. Tears gathered in her eyes. The young black cop thrust a large white handkerchief into her hand before any of us could move. Mr. Benton placed one hand lightly on her shoulder, patted it gently, then even more gently tipped her face toward him.

"Please," he signed, "don't be afraid. No one will hurt you. Please tell me, Mary. Why were you on the parkway?"

"Walking, just walking. Not do anything bad! Not bad girl."

"Of course not. We know that," Mr. Benton told her quickly. "But why were you there?"

"Run away!" Mary signed. "Home bad. Not my real parents. Not nice. Not good. Talk! Talk! Talk! Lips move and move. Not understand! Try tell them sign. Please sign. They not understand me. No. Never use sign. Lonely. So lonely there."

"School, Mary. Did you go to school?" Mr. Benton asked.

"School same!" Mary signed, tossing her head back scornfully. "Talk. All day talk with lips! Say sign no good. Teachers say sign language is sin language! No! Not true! I want learn. But hard. Very, very hard. I try. When I talk, sound not right. No one understand. So . . . why talk? All kids sign when teacher can't see. Easier. Make-believe all time, then teachers happy.

"But not good. Learn only little that way. Hate school! Hate house. Alone. Lonely." A wistful look erased the anger briefly. Her hands moved slowly, tenderly. "Had Buddy . . . he love me!"

Buddy? Who was Buddy? Seeing the question on our faces, Mary continued, her face soft. "Buddy dog. *My* dog. Little, brown and white. Soft, long ears." She screwed her face into a mournful expression, tilted her face down, and pulled her hands down from her own ears, showing us how Buddy looked. Then she slumped back, arms hanging limp, telling us with her face and hands and body, "Buddy die."

Straightening, she stared defiantly at Mr. Benton again and announced, "Sad. Home not nice. Run away. Think job find maybe? Other place. Clean, cook good, sew very good. Run. Run away!"

She'd hitched to the parkway and gotten several lifts. When she hadn't talked to the man who'd picked her up at the service area near Norwalk, he'd dropped her off near the Millport exit. In the dark she'd stumbled into a tree and hit her head. Dazed, she picked herself up and headed for the exit. It was at that point that the state troopers had found her.

"Please, don't send me back!" Mary pleaded with Mr. Benton urgently, rubbing her fingers along her wrists. She wasn't signing now, just watching Mr. Benton and Kathy talking. They'd turned away. I couldn't catch the discussion now; it was all too fast. I stepped closer to Mary, wanting to say something to reassure her somehow, and saw her wet a finger and touch her wrist again. As she moved her fingers away, I saw the red welts and bruised skin clearly.

"Joe, Mr. Benton, Kathy, please! Please look at her wrists!" I burst out. "They're rubbed raw!"

Everyone, startled, turned and stared at Mary's arms. Joe, who was nearest, dropped to his knees, pointed to her wrists gently, then quickly signed: "Mary, your arms? How? What happened? Who hurt you?"

Mary pulled back and thrust both hands behind her. Her eyes searched our faces. For long moments she sat mute.

"Please . . . please tell us!" Joe pleaded.

Her lips quivering, she pulled her hands forward, signing very slowly: "Ran away before. They tie me to chair. To stop me running away."

Like a sudden blast of icy wind, her words lashed us. Our eyes widened with shock. No one moved or tried to speak.

Mr. Benton recovered first. He whirled to face the stunned policeman, spoke and signed urgently, angrily. "You can't take her back to these people! People? They're animals!"

Neither of the men gave him an argument. Wearily the older cop stretched out both arms and asked, "No, but what can we do? We can call the local police. They will get in touch with the proper agency. After that, well . . ."

"No, wait," Mr. Benton said, struggling for control, pulling a card from his wallet. "Why not call the Connecticut Commission for the Deaf? They have a twenty-four-hour-a-day emergency interpreter service. Inform them. They'll help you handle it."

"Yeah!" the younger cop exclaimed, his relief plain. "That's exactly what we'll do, right, Tom?" At his partner's nod he grabbed the phone.

"Mr. Benton, all of you, thanks a million," Tom said. "We're sorry, we just didn't know how to handle this."

"I understand," Mr. Benton told him. "Most people don't. But that's changing. We're working on it." He handed them a small pamphlet. "Here, take this, too, please. It shows a few basic signs and the manual alphabet. It will help you recognize a deaf person in the future."

"Thanks again," Tom said. "Don't know what we'd have done without you. Thank God that therapist from the speech and hearing department of Millport Hospital gave us your name. God knows I've seen a lot, but—How can a thing like this happen?"

Mr. Benton sighed wearily, raised his eyebrows high. He stood silently for a long moment as if searching for words. "Well, Officer," he said at last, "having a handicapped child is no picnic. It's rough as hell on parents, on families. Sometimes they don't know how to deal with it. So some parents just reject their handicapped children. They're ashamed and hide them away. Some overprotect them. Mary's people are foster parents. It's hard to find people to take a child who is 'different.' Somebody just figured wrong. It happens." He turned away from the policemen, lit a cigarette, then faced Mary once more and explained everything to her.

She reached out and squeezed his hand. Her eyes swept our faces and made sure we were all watching, and she smiled bravely. "Thank you!" she signed. "Okay now. Good-bye."

Joe took my hand and held it tight all the way home. I sat close, still shaken, knowing I'd never forget a floppy-eared dog I'd never seen, the flying fingers that chased the fear away from a pale, terrified face, or a small girl called Mary.

19

■ "Did you take Oliver in for his shots yet?" Dad asked as we relaxed after Sunday dinner several weeks later.

"He'll get them next week," I answered.

"Next thing you know, he'll be a full-grown cat, a real lady-killer. We'll have to have him altered."

"Must we?"

"Yup. Or he'll spray everything in sight to let the girls know he's available. Besides taking off nights gallivanting and getting into fights," Dad replied firmly.

"I know. Joe's cat nearly got his leg torn off one night before they had him altered. As it is, he'll limp for the rest of his life. He's okay now, though, and stays home nights." I patted Oliver regretfully. "Sorry, Oliver," I told him. "That's the way it's gotta be."

No one spoke for a couple of minutes, a rare occurrence in our house. Something was up, I could sense it, see it, too; there was that uneasy "who's going to broach the subject?" look on their faces. I waited. Finally, Mom got it out. "Jenny, honey, aren't you seeing quite a lot of Joe? I mean . . . Joe's a very nice boy, but—"

"But what?" Not quite sure why, I flared up suddenly. "Since when have you ever told me whom I should be friends with? You've *never* tried to pick my friends! What's wrong with Joe? He's been a—a godsend, you know that!"

What's going on here anyway? I thought. They liked Joe, I knew that.

"Jennifer," Dad said, "we don't have any objection to Joe. He's a fine young man."

"So?"

"But," he continued, "maybe you shouldn't see so much of any one boy."

"Are you afraid it's getting to be a thing with us? Too serious? Is that what's bothering you?"

"Sort of," Mom admitted.

"For Pete's sake, that's silly! We're just friends, very good friends, that's all." (Who tells parents everything?)

The look they gave each other made further comment unnecessary. They *were* worried. "Listen, there's nothing to worry about, honest! Sure, I like Joe an awful lot. Wait a minute. Are you upset because it's hard to understand him? Because he's got a 'deaf voice'? *I* understand him; you would, too, if you could lip-read or sign. Or is it because he's deaf? Is *that* it?" I demanded.

"Jennifer," my father said, "that's not it! We just think it would be good for you to be with hearing people more, to keep up with your lip-reading, with others—to live in the *whole* world. After all, we live in a hearing world."

"*You* live in a hearing world! I don't! Not any more. Joe doesn't; Barbara doesn't; neither do millions of other people! Sure, we live among other people who hear, and the easier it is for us to communicate with others, the better. But communication is a two-way street!"

"We know," my father agreed hastily.

145

"*Do* you? People who hear are so often uncomfortable with us, with anyone who is *different* really. When I sense that, when it's very hard to understand, I often just let it go or bluff it through rather than ask them to repeat or explain again and again. Then *I* feel lousy because I don't know what I've missed or whether it was important! It's hard for hearing people to communicate honestly with us, so few even try to."

"We do," my mother said.

"Sure *you* do, but most people don't know where to begin, so they don't even try. *They* feel pity, guilt, and discomfort, while *we* feel apart, left out, rejected, alien!"

The stricken look on my mother's face nearly stopped me, but I stumbled on.

"You know, I've always loved being with people, but when you're deaf, it can be so frustrating! Doing things alone, not *trying* to communicate is a lot easier. When I'm reading or writing or working on something I care about, I'm neither deaf nor lonely. When I'm with you or Joe or Donna or Barbara and we communicate easily, I'm just like everyone else!

"Look, I've found out that I can concentrate a lot harder than people with all five senses and often think things through better, too. I've learned to enjoy being alone, but you can't be alone *all* the time. Everyone needs someone to talk to, to listen to, to share ideas, questions, and experiences with; to touch, to learn from, to laugh and cry with, to love . . . that's what being human is all about!"

They both flinched; my mother shut her eyes for a moment. Then, taking my hands in his, my father spoke: "Well said, Jennifer. Go on."

146

"Don't you see? I need *people*; everybody does! I have to be with those who accept me, who communicate with me or will try to. Whether it's by lip-reading, sign, or writing doesn't matter; whether they are hearing or deaf doesn't matter either!" I took another deep breath. "As for Joe," I finished, "he's . . . he's the best thing that's happened to me in a long time! He's warm and kind and patient and bright as hell! He's—he's wonderful!"

Neither of my parents said anything. I searched their faces, determined to defend Joe against all comers anywhere, anytime . . . forever! My mother's face softened. "Yes, of course, he is, honey," she said. "Now, about school. Jenny, you'll be going back to Stevens very soon. The spring semester starts February first, and you'll finish the year with the rest of your class. We all feel you're ready to go back now."

February 1! That was less than a month away! It had been so long, almost a year, and now they were saying I could finally go back. Why wasn't I thrilled to pieces? This was what I had been waiting for, what I wanted so badly. Why was there a cold lump in my chest? Why was I suddenly scared to death?

"Uh, it's not that simple," I said. "There's something strange going on in this town. I asked Joe about school."

"And?" my father prompted.

I told them. When I'd finished filling them in on all the details, their faces were grim.

"It's a conspiracy! A conspiracy of silence!" I yelled my voice out of control now: I only realized and lowered it when Mom moved her hand down swiftly. "Everybody's in on it! The kids understand so little and don't let on; the teachers and administrators either don't know or don't say or don't want to know!"

Mom's face was flushed, her mouth tight; her anger matched mine. "We know, Jenny. Dad and I had a conference last week with Mr. Patterson, head of the Speech and Hearing Department, Mrs. Gardner, and Mrs. Foster, the teacher who teaches the hearing-impaired at Stevens, about your individual educational plan. Every hearing-impaired student is required to have one by law."

"Oh. That's when it was decided then?"

"Yes. But when I asked Mr. Patterson if the kids could understand in regular classes of twenty-five or more without interpreters, he said he *assumed* they did! He was very charming, but smug and cold as ice, that man! But, Jenny, you *must* go back to school."

They meant it.

"You *must*, honey," my father said grimly.

"No!" I screamed. "It's crazy! It would be torture! I *won't* understand anything! No! I won't, and you can't make me!"

I couldn't look at them anymore. I couldn't sit there another minute. Jumping up, I ran to the closet and grabbed my jacket. As I turned, I noticed Mom's car keys on the hall table. I thrust them into my pocket and ran to the garage.

Quickly, before either of them could stop me, I started the car and drove off.

My head was pounding; tears of pure rage sprang from my eyes. I rubbed them away. It was wrong. All wrong! I'd tried so hard for so long. I wanted to go to school, but to a school where I could learn. This wouldn't work. They knew that! Then why? Why, knowing that, did they say I had to go? To go back and sit there like . . . like a dummy most of the time! I'd go crazy trying to keep up in a large class. I couldn't.

I drove on and on, confused, frightened, trapped by questions no one seemed to have any good answers to. My parents had let me down. I *couldn't* go back. Then where could I go? Where? Whom could I turn to now?

Joe was away. The Bentons wouldn't be home until tomorrow, he'd said. Frantic, wanting someone to talk to desperately, I turned around and drove quickly to Donna's house.

Donna wasn't home. Her mother told me she'd gone to a rock concert with some of the kids from school. As I got back into the car, I remembered. She told me about it weeks ago. I'd forgotten.

Barbara lived way over on the other side of town. Better not . . . getting late . . . ought to go back. Damn it, there just wasn't anywhere to go, anyone to turn to. Everything had gone wrong. What could I do? What?

Almost too late, I braked sharply as the light just ahead turned red. A black car shot in front of me from a side road. I'd stopped in time, but only just in time! Missed hitting it by inches. Jolted, badly shaken, I clutched the wheel as I waited for the light to change. Whew! That had been close. Too close!

When the green flashed on again, I eased my foot onto the accelerator, relaxed my hands on the wheel, and headed home.

The trouble with our house is that anyone who enters can be seen immediately by anyone in the living room.

So any plan I'd had for sneaking upstairs would work only if no one were waiting for me there. This was highly unlikely under the circumstances. Not being able to make myself invisible at will, I braced myself for the upcoming scene.

Three people rushed to me before I got my coat off. My mother simply hugged me hard, as if she hadn't been sure she'd ever see me again. I handed over the car keys silently.

My father glared at me, then spoke very carefully with barely controlled rage: "Jennifer, don't you *ever*, ever do that again! Understand?"

"Yes," I told him. "I'm sorry." I stared at *Joe*, who, standing behind them, looked very grim.

"Hi!" I said "What are you doing here? I thought you weren't coming back until tomorrow."

"We left early," he replied. "I came over to tell you that my early applications to several colleges came through."

"Oh! Which ones?"

His irrepressible grin broke through as he named them. "I've been accepted by Gallaudet, by the National Technical Institute of the Deaf, by the Rochester Institute of Technology, by California State University at Northridge, and by Columbia University."

"Oh, Joe, that's *wonderful!*" I shrieked, hugging him.

"Yeah," he said, breaking away abruptly. "Jenny, come inside and sit down. I want to talk to you!"

We sat in a rough semicircle, Mom at my side, where she could see Joe best. She could lip-read him a little. I noticed the pad on the table was covered with his writing, phrases he'd had to clarify for them. He must have been waiting with them for quite a while.

Joe looked at me sternly and said, "Jenny, you *must* go back to school!"

"Oh, no, not you, too! Joe, I can't."

"You can!" he insisted.

"You don't understand. You think you know everything. You're terribly bright but—"

He cut me off quickly, something he rarely did. "*So are you*, Jenny!"

That stopped me cold, his saying it straight out like that. He pressed on, his eyes narrowed, his anger plain. Yet he spoke and signed with his usual control and care with me.

"You can!" he repeated. "You have to! I didn't think you were a quitter or a coward. Grow up and think straight, Jenny! Stop running away. Stop acting like a spoiled kid. You can't have it all your own way. All right. There *are* some things we *can't* have, can't do. You have to accept that and concentrate on the things we *can* do."

"You don't *really* understand!" I screamed. "*You've* never known anything else!"

"No, I haven't." he paused briefly, then said, gently, "Okay. It's a lot harder for you. You haven't been deaf that long. I've lived with deafness all my life, and *everything* that goes with it."

Involuntarily I closed my eyes, as if by not seeing, I could shut out the truth, the pain.

Joe's fingers touched my face gently as he demanded, "Look at me! Don't shut me out! Look at me, Jenny! What do *you want?*" he asked.

I lifted my head and opened my eyes. Giving me no chance to answer, he continued furiously. "Damn it, Jenny, I never said it would be easy! But deaf people have gone to school with everybody else for more than a hundred years! You act like nobody ever did it before! You say you want to *do* things—help change things. If that's what you *really* want, then use your head! If you're going to throw away the advantages of having been able to hear for almost sixteen years, then you're a fool! If you cop out now, you really are deaf *and* dumb —*and* you'll never be anything else!"

With a final scorching look, he grabbed his jacket and slammed out of the house.

I just sat there stunned, ashamed. He was right. I had no other option. But it was going to be so frustrating. So terribly hard . . .

My mother touched me gently. "Honey, you ran out before we could finish, before we could tell you."

"Tell me what?" I asked, not yet fully recovered from Joe's blast.

"There's a law, Jenny, remember?" my father said. "We're *not* going to accept your individual educational plan. Patterson and the rest, except for Mrs. Gardner, don't understand your needs, but we do. You're entitled by law to an interpreter and an 'appropriate' program."

"Great! So I'm entitled. If *they* don't understand, how am I going to get it?" I demanded.

Mom answered that one. "First I'll talk to Mr. Engels, who is in charge of special education. He may not realize just what's going on. If that doesn't work, I'll go straight to Dr. Peters!"

Dr. Peters was our superintendent of schools and

Mom's boss, although most of the staff rarely saw him.

"But won't that get you in trouble?"

"Maybe, but I don't think so, Jenny. At any rate, that's not relevant. It's got to be done."

My father nodded in agreement, then said slowly, "It's not just *you* or Millport, Jenny. There are thousands of towns all over the country doing the same thing. Mainstreaming without really knowing how to go about it! We'll put on all the pressure we can. If all that doesn't work, we'll sue! Take our lawsuit right up to the Supreme Court if necessary! We'd have plenty of backing and help from the National Center for Law and the Deaf *and* the deaf community."

Knowing my father, I'd bet on that. Obviously they'd been checking everything out from the beginning. They told me they'd been in contact and talking with other parents, with the Bentons and other deaf leaders all over the country. They'd been working and fighting for me all along.

"It'll be rough, but you'll get the services you need, Jenny," my mother insisted. "If you have to, you can go to a private school. We'll do everything we can. You can count on that. The rest is up to you."

It figured. I wasn't fighting this battle alone. I never had been. I should have known that. But then I'm stupid sometimes—just like everybody else.

The chilling fog of confusion and fear slid away. We all breathed easily once more.

Abruptly, breaking the calm, my mother's eyebrows rose, her mouth dropped open. "Oh, I forgot!" she said. She reached into her handbag and after a hasty search produced a large white envelope. "This came for you this morning, Jenny," she announced, handing it to me.

"It's from Mr. Stein," I told them. "They're going to feature my poem in a special issue of the *Clarion!* He says he's proud of me and looks forward to having me back."

"What poem, honey?" my father asked.

"I wrote it a couple of weeks ago. It's a Sign-Poem. It's called 'Unchained.'"

"Tell us, show us!" he said.

"Okay. It goes like this:

> *No prison can hold us*
> *Though silence enfold us*
> *All, all can be told us*
> *Through these, Sign and Words.*
>
> *Sign and Words mean Learning*
> *Sign and Words mean Knowing*
> *Sign and Words mean Touching*
> *Sign and Words mean Caring*
> *Sign and Words mean Sharing*
> *Sign and Words are you and me*
> *Being free!*
> *And*
> *Free to be!*

They beamed. The tenderness on their faces began to get to me. I was about to cry when my mother rescued me. "Jenny, that's lovely. Did you write it for Joe?"

"No, I wrote it for Mr. Stein. But I . . . I wrote it for Joe, too. . . . Dad . . . you wouldn't consider letting me use the car for just a little while, would you? I want to see Joe, to tell him—"

Dad pressed the keys into my hand and kissed me on the cheek. I squeezed his hand and ran toward the door. This time I knew where I was going. I knew what I had to do.